# The Glam Rock Murders

Andrew Hickey

## BY THE SAME AUTHOR:

### Non-Fiction

Sci-Ence! Justice Leak!

The Beatles In Mono

The Beach Boys On CD: vol 1 - 1961-1969

The Beach Boys On CD: vol 2 - 1970-2011

An Incomprehensible Condition:An Unauthorised Guide To Grant Morrison's Seven Soldiers

Monkee Music

Preservation: The Kinks' Music 1964-1974

California Dreaming: The LA Pop Music Scene and the 1960s

The Black Archive: The Mind Robber

Welcome to the Multiverse: An Unauthorised Guide to Grant Morrison's Multiversity (ebook only)

Fifty Stories for Fifty Years: An Unauthorised Look at Doctor Who

### Fiction

Ideas and Entities (short stories)

Faction Paradox: Head of State

Doctor Watson Investigates: The Curse of the Scarlet Neckerchief (ebook only)

Destroyer: A Black Magic Story

The Basilisk Murders: A Sarah Turner Mystery

For Holly

# Contents

# Rock and Roll, Part 1

"Okay, let's try it again"

The opening riff of "Misty Lady" rang out from Sid Berry's guitar, and even though I was never a fan of the Cillas, I couldn't help tapping my foot along with it. When you've heard a song that many times, on the radio, on TV, in the background in pubs, you can't help but nod along.

"Ooh, ooh ooh, my misty misty... stop. Stop. Terry, what the fuck are you doing?"

"What's the matter?"

Graham Stewart, the Cillas' vocalist, had thrown down his mic and stormed over to their bass player.

"Terry, it goes G to D to D diminished seventh to A minor. You were playing a fucking C. Where in that sequence does a C fit in?"

"Well, you can play a C in the A minor."

Graham turned puce. "Well, you can, if you think playing the fucking third of the chord in the bass is in any way acceptable. But also, you weren't playing it on the A minor, were you? You were playing it in the D dim seven. You *arse*."

Hi, I'm Sarah Turner. You may remember me from such serial murders as that time those technolibertarians all got murdered on that island. Not that I killed them – though I was tempted – but I solved the murders.

Anyway, when I'm not solving crimes like some ace Miss Marple-style supersleuth, I'm a journalist, and I was currently watching the first rehearsal of the "legendary" 70s glam rock group the Cillas, before they started their reunion tour. At the time, I thought it was likely

9

to be a fairly boring assignment, but I didn't realise that murder had started to follow me around like I was some kind of a Jessica Fletcher.

So we're going to get into another story of how I solved terrible crimes (unless I didn't and I'm the murderer this time – woo, suspense!) (spoiler, I'm not the murderer) but at the time I was just thinking what an annoying bunch of arseholes this band were, especially the lead singer. I needed the money I was making from being there, but I was beginning to wonder if I needed it quite enough to put up with all this mantitlement.

To set the scene, this was a rehearsal room in Clacton, in the early afternoon. Big, empty, echoey room with no atmosphere at all. Whitewashed concrete walls, high ceilings. The band were arranged as they would be on stage. Graham Stewart was at a mic up front, wearing tight leather trousers, with a grey mullet and goatee beard that made him look like a cross between Peter Stringfellow and Noel Edmonds.

Directly behind him were Terry Pattison, a bald, fat, little white bloke in T-shirt and jeans, playing bass, and Sid Berry, a skinny black bloke with short salt-and-pepper hair, about a foot taller than Terry, on guitar. The two of them together looked like a number 10 come to life. In between them, and set slightly back again, was Pete Le Mesurier, the drummer. Younger than the rest of them, in his mid sixties rather than early seventies, he had a square, grey, face.

And off to the sides were three younger musicians. On my left as I faced the band was my wife, Jane, on keyboards. Behind her was Simon Cotton, playing a second drum kit, while on my far right was his brother Andy Cotton on a second guitar. All three of these were white, in their twenties, and looking bored, as well as seeming far more professional than the old men.

There were a few other people in there as well – a fat white bloke in his thirties with a goatee beard who seemed to be a professional fan, a few roadies, and various wives, business people, and assorted hangers-on. While you and I may not have thought about the Cillas in decades, except when hearing their tracks on Radio 2 or seeing them on "I Love Nostalgic Cheap Clips of the 70s with Stuart Maconie Mocking Them" on Channel Four, apparently they were still big enough business that it was worth them having all sorts of people in the room doing nothing other than getting in the way.

If I was playing with my old band for the first time in forty years, I'd want to do it in private, but then I'm not a rock star, and don't have that kind of ego that wants to be in front of an audience at all times.

Sid lit a cigarette while Graham was shouting at Terry, apparently unaware of laws against smoking in the workplace. Within seconds, I could feel my chest starting to tighten and hurt – I'm allergic to tobacco smoke – and wished I'd brought my inhaler along. Graham, however, seemed oblivious to everything except his anger at the bass player.

"Look, Terry, it's very simple. You play the root notes on the G and D, do a little walk up on the diminished seventh, and then play the fifth on the A minor. It's not like it's a hard part or anything. I can play it and I don't play an instrument."

"Well, why don't you play it then? If it's so easy, you can play bass rather than poncing about like a wanker at the front of the stage waving your arms, can't you? Or you could at least just talk about it instead of giving me a bollocking for a wrong note."

Graham sighed. "Okay, I'm sorry. I know you've not played live in a long time..."

"Since you sacked me."

"Okay, yes, since I sacked you..."

"Since you sacked me from my band, which I formed..."

The other members of the Cillas were looking on with some amusement at Graham's increasing discomfort. I'd not met the band before, but it was already obvious that their *prima donna* lead singer was not the most popular person in Cillaworld.

"Okay... just, you know what, forget it. Play whatever the fuck you like."

Graham walked back to his mic, and picked it up. Andy Cotton, the band's musical director, lifted his right hand from the acoustic guitar he was holding and started beating time. "All right, everyone, third time's the charm. 'Misty' from the top. One, two, three, four."

Jane looked over at me as the song started up again, and rolled her eyes. I smiled. I'd heard plenty of stories about Graham from her before, and it seemed they were all true. But in case he had a point, I paid attention to what Terry was doing on the bass – I couldn't really help it anyway, given the way the throbbing from the low notes was disturbing my stomach – and it sounded absolutely fine to me. Possibly not the greatest bass playing I'd ever heard, but musical enough

They got as far as the middle eight before they got into serious trouble and ground to a halt. Once again, it was Terry who was making the mistakes.

"It's okay, Terry," said Sid. "That part there was always a bastard to play. To get it right you have to fret the two strings and play them both simultaneously, then pull off and quickly fret the eleventh fret, but just get the harmonic, not the actual note. It's not really a bass part at all in the conventional sense. I was showing off, basically."

Terry nodded. "I'll probably get it eventually, it's just I'm not Jaco bloody Pastorius, you know?"

Andy walked over and conferred with Jane for a second, then turned to the others.

"Okay, I think I have a solution," he said. "Jane's only using one hand on that section anyway, so if you can just do the fiddly top bit, Terry, she can hold down the main bassline with all the root notes. Make sense?"

Terry nodded, cautiously. "I'd rather just do the bassline and have her do the fiddly bit..."

"Can't work that way, I'm afraid. Those harmonics and glisses aren't something you can do on a keyboard."

"Fair enough."

"Okay," said Andy, "let's try this once more."

And the band played through their glam rock hit from forty-five years earlier, without a hitch.

I needed a drink, but there didn't appear to be any alcohol in the rehearsal room. I'd talked to Jane about it at a break earlier, and she'd told me that Graham had asked that the room be kept clear of all alcoholic or caffeinated drinks, because he was a Mormon. I sighed at this diva wanting to exert a little power over the rest of us, but I was resigned to my fate.

But it didn't seem right to be listening to this music, which I was only really familiar with from drunken family parties, without a half-drunk can of cheap lager in my hand. There was a cognitive dissonance here, hearing such familiar music in such a different circumstance.

I looked over in the corner, and saw two middle-aged women having a stand-up, yelling, fight. That was more like it. That was exactly
what I needed to see when I heard "Misty Lady." I was at home again.

# Solid Gold, Easy Action

So, at this point you're probably wondering why I was hanging around in rehearsals with a band I don't even like. Well, to tell you the truth, I was wondering that myself.

I can't say it was exactly the job I'd have wanted to take at that point, but when you're a freelancer you take whatever work you can get, and that was all that was available at the time. I needed money, they needed a writer.

You'd think maybe that after I'd helped catch a billionaire who'd killed two people, there would have been a bit of a market for me as a journalist. You'd think wrong. If you become known as someone who pisses off billionaires, what happens is that no-one will touch you with someone else's bargepole, in case you piss off another one.

Right now, billionaires have the ability, and in many cases the desire, to close down anywhere that employs writers with a frivolous lawsuit. Everyone remembers what happened to Gawker, and no-one wants to repeat that (though my own personal view is that if you go posting people's stolen sex tapes online you're a sex criminal and deserve to be shut down, but my view is very much a minority one in the journalism world, apparently). So I was *persona non grata* among everyone who could give me work. I couldn't even get anything on Upwork.

But on the other hand, I did still have one way of getting work – I was married to Jane Simpson, and Jane just happens to be the best session keyboard player working in the country today. So when the Cillas reformed and needed to get some people who could actually play to act as their backing band, she got the job.

15

Jane had played in Graham Stewart's backing band on his last tour, and he'd liked her – which in Graham Stewart world meant that he'd completely ignored her at all times, trusting that she'd just get on with her job. She knew most of the repertoire, because half of it was in his solo set, and she wasn't doing anything else, so she'd been hired along with Stewart's drummer Simon Cotton and Simon's brother Andy, who was playing guitar.

Now you might be wondering, since the Cillas were, you know, a band, who played their own instruments, why they would want to hire other people to play the guitar, keyboards, and drums. The sad fact is that most of the bands from the 60s and 70s who get back together do this. Half of them are out of practice and haven't played for twenty or more years, and the other half are so old that arthritis is making it impossible for them to play the parts. So when you go and see [Redacted] or [band my lawyers have advised me to cut out of the book], what you're actually seeing is two or three old blokes largely miming while other people play the parts.

So the Cillas themselves were playing their parts, but they had stunt musicians to cover them in case they fucked up too badly, and to fill in for the dead member (only one in the Cillas' case, their original lead guitarist Ray Evans – they'd been quite lucky in terms of mortality rate, compared to most bands of their age), and generally to make them sound like they were a band rather than a bunch of amateurs.

At least in the Cillas' case they were singing their own parts. That had always been their gimmick, the way they stood out from the other glam rock bands. While T-Rex were being all fey and Slade all shouty, the Cillas had been the only band of their era who regularly did four- or five-part harmony vocals. Graham Stewart was the lead singer, but Robert Michaels, the rhythm guitarist, would usually double his vocal, while the others would sing intertwining vocal harmonies. Michaels wasn't on this tour, because he was busy being a famously reclusive mad genius somewhere, but three of the other 70s band members from the band's various lineups (the ones that hadn't died, got religion, or both) were with Stewart, and between them they were able to do a passable recreation of the band's old vocal sound.

But anyway, this was a massive reunion tour, for the band's fiftieth anniversary, and the thing about massive tours is that they need a vast amount of text generating. You need press releases, tour programmes, social media updates, you need someone to come up with witty lines to feed the band members so they can trot them out in interviews. You need, in short, someone who can write a thousand words of usable copy in an hour on demand. You need me, or someone like me.

And so Jane had suggested me for the role. Officially I was a PR assistant, but my actual role was text generator. I needed the money, and this seemed an easy way to get that. It also allowed me to spend more time with my wife, which was something else I needed after the emotional roller-coaster we'd been through earlier in 2018.

And speaking of wives, that was who the two women who had been screaming at each other, and who had once again caused the rehearsal to grind to a halt, were. I'd not been able to hear the argument, but unlike the arguments that usually arose in my family while that music was playing, this one wasn't about what you'd said to our Shirl at our Vicky's wedding, but seemed to be about business matters.

Eventually, the argument seemed to be settled in favour of Kate Michaels, the wife of Robert Michaels, the band's former rhythm guitarist. Robert hadn't wanted to join the reunion, Jane had told me, but he still owned a share in the Cillas' corporation, and had sent his wife along to make sure his business interests weren't compromised. Very glam. Much rock and roll.

Kate Michaels was in her late forties, as best I could tell, but her face showed several signs of not-particularly-wonderful cosmetic surgery, so I couldn't be sure. She was dressed younger than her age, and had bleach-blonde hair and a determined look on her face.

She marched over to Andy and said to him in a strong Scouse accent "you're the one in charge of the setlist, am I right?"

"Yep, that's me. Is there anything about it you'd like to talk about?"

"Why have you got 'Laguna Beach' and 'Nightlife Skyline' in there? They're not Cillas songs."

He became slightly more formal in his body language, standing up a little straighter and looking her in the eye. "Well, we thought that since they're Graham's biggest hits, the audience would want to hear them."

"I don't give a shit about what's Graham's hits. This isn't a Graham Stewart show, it's a Cillas show."

"Of course, but..."

"If you went to see the Beatles, would you expect them to do the bloody Frog song?"

Andy started to explain to her, but Andy was one of those kinds of people who would never miss an opportunity to pedantically correct someone on an utterly unimportant point of trivia, so he had to start with "It wasn't actually called the Frog song, that's a common misconception. It was actually called..."

"I don't *care* what it was actually called. What I care about is that this is supposed to be a Cillas tour, and my husband wrote the Cillas songs. You know the license terms – all songs performed have to be Cillas songs. Graham Stewart wasn't the only bloody member of the band, you know."

While this was going on, the other woman in the fight had come across to chat to me. This was Janine Stewart, Graham's wife. She was dark-haired, skinny, and much more modestly dressed than Kate, completely covered from her shoulders to her knees, but despite that she didn't seem especially proper – something about her face suggested to me she was up for a laugh, and I liked her immediately. I suppose even Mormons can cut loose occasionally – and after all, she was a professional dancer.

"Of course, you know why she doesn't want them doing those songs?" she said to me.

"No, why?" I responded, because it seemed expected of me, though I was pretty sure I knew.

"They're not Robert's songs, so she won't make any money from them, like she does when they play them. It's why she wouldn't let them do their cover version of 'Rock Around the Clock' either."

"But that was their biggest hit!"

"I know, but it doesn't make money for the genius Robert Michaels, so out it goes." She grinned, wryly. "I suppose that's why they call him a genius. He's figured out a way to make money from other people going out and working every night."

"I fucking heard that!" came the Liverpudlian-accented cry from the other side of the room.

"Oh God, here it comes," said Janine, as she prepared herself for round two of the fight.

# This Town Ain't Big Enough for Both of Us

"What the fuck are you saying about me and my husband?" Kate was saying, as she stormed over

At the time of the row, I had no idea why there was such enmity between these two women. I later discovered from Jane that the main reason was that Janine Stewart had been employed as a dancer on the tour against the wishes of Kate Michaels.

Now, before you get the wrong idea, I want to say two things. Firstly, I'm about as good a judge of whether someone's a competent dancer as I am of their ability to translate from proto-Finno-Ugric into Basque. And secondly, Janine Stewart had been a professional dancer for years before she'd met Graham. So I'm not going to take a stand on whether she was good enough to do the job or not.

But some people involved in the tour thought she wasn't, and not least among them was Kate. I'd missed out on all the drama between them that had gone into making the tour happen, but it was instantly clear that these two people were never going to be best of friends.

"I'm sorry, Kate dear," said Janine, as sweetly as only someone who wants to commit murder possibly can, "but could you explain why you're making all these suggestions to the creative side of the tour? After all, you're only involved in the business side, and we artists do need the space to grow and experiment away from critical eyes."

Kate was not having any of this pretending to be polite shit. "I'm getting involved, Janine, because I'm protecting my investment and that of my husband — you know, the one who was actually creative and who wrote all these songs the band are playing? I need to make sure that the show doesn't devalue the Cillas' name by putting some half-baked shit out there."

"Devalue the Cillas' name? No-one even remembers the Cillas except as Graham's old band. And half his fans don't even know he was ever in a band."

"What fans would these be? The ones who got Graham's last tour cancelled because of lack of ticket sales? Or the ones who didn't buy his last three albums so the record label dropped him? Maybe the ones who voted him off *Strictly* in the first round? Would those be the fans you mean?"

Janine's face was starting to turn purple, and Graham stepped in. "Look, love, Kate's only doing her job. She's got to look after Robert, because God knows he's not capable of looking after himself. He needs his share of the money – he's certainly not done any actual work in the last thirty years. Let Kate make her suggestions if that's what will keep her happy."

The astonishing thing is that I think he actually believed he was being helpful and tactful – this was what would pass for tact in Graham Stewart's dealings with anyone who wasn't a star.

So of course both women turned on him, in what became a three-way screaming match between them all.

From the looks on the faces of Graham's bandmates, this was clearly business as usual. Sid stubbed his cigarette out on one of Pete's snare drums while Pete wasn't looking, and then the six of them chatted among themselves. I couldn't hear what they were saying, but Andy was demonstrating some chord changes to the others, and Jane picked out a couple of notes on the keyboard, then nodded as if to say "yes, got it."

While all this was going on, the bloke who was sat next to me, and who I'd not paid much attention to before that point, turned to me. This was a white bloke, maybe in his late thirties, and probably weighing a good twenty stone. Big bloke. He had a close-cropped beard that I guessed was to cover up his multiple chins, and he was wearing a baseball cap with the Cillas' logo on it.

His name, I was later to find out (he wasn't the kind of person who bothered with introductions), was Chuck Bentley, and he was a fan who'd managed to get himself a position on the tour as an unofficial fan advisor.

He said to me, in what I think he thought was a friendly, conspiratorial, tone "Don't you just hate it when the wives get themselves involved?"

I looked at him. "I'm here because I'm a wife. I'm married to Jane, the keyboard player."

He paused for a second as he mentally recalibrated, and I was pleased to see that the lesbomisic comment he was apparently considering didn't actually get as far as his mouth.

"Oh, you know what I mean though. Wives interfering in the creative process. It's Yoko Ono syndrome."

"You mean when a respected conceptual artist and musician decides to introduce her husband to *avant-garde* and Dadaist art practices, increasing his artistic toolbox and inspiring his period of greatest creativity?"

"Oh, you know what I mean." He turned away, annoyed that I wasn't planning to join in with his misogyny.

The sad thing was, though, that I did indeed know what he meant.

Graham, Janine, and Kate continued their argument, the eventual upshot of which was that Kate would remain a dancer in the show, but that Graham's solo material would be cut, although Janine eventually agreed that the band could play a snatch of 'Laguna Beach' as Graham walked on stage in the encore.

Graham went back to the other musicians, and explained the situation to them. Andy pulled out a pen and struck lines through the songs on the setlist.

"So what we going to do instead? 'Rock Around the Clock'?" Andy asked.

Graham looked nervously over at Kate. "No, originals only, I think."

"Good" Chuck muttered, next to me.

"What was that?" I asked him, more out of politeness than interest.

"Good, no-one wants to hear cover versions. We're there to hear Robert Michaels' songs."

"But wasn't 'Rock Around the Clock' a number one hit for them?" I asked, confused. "Surely their fans want to hear their hits?"

"Oh, well, if you're talking about the casuals, I suppose," he said, waving his hand dismissively. "But the real fans are there for higher things than just hearing the touring jukebox."

As the band started up their rendition of one of their number one hits, I did wonder if the Cillas themselves thought that, but I said nothing.

One thing I hadn't realised until turning up to this rehearsal was how many of the Cillas' songs I actually knew. This was a band I'd barely heard of, but it turns out that there were at least a dozen of their songs whose tunes I was familiar with. The one they were playing now, "Yer Mama's Calling Me ", was one of those. I don't know where I'd heard it from – probably an advert, or maybe in the Muzak in a restaurant or something – but it turned out that even though I'd never consciously listened to it, I knew all the tune and most of the words already.

You probably don't recognise the name, even though it was number one for one week in 1973, but you'd know it if you heard it. It's the one that goes:

"Little lady I can hear you talking, but you're gonna have to let me be

There's only you and her who've got my number, and your mama's calling me

Little lady, there's no use in squawking, cos one and one and one makes three "

And only gets more disgusting from there.

Still, despite everything, I found myself singing along. After they'd finished the run-through, I turned to look at Chuck, and saw him stone-faced in silence.

"What's the matter?" I asked, "I thought you loved this band."

"I do," he said, "which is why I don't like to see them debasing themselves like this. This... *bubblegum* nonsense... that's not what the Cillas are about. It's like if the Beatles were going to reform and do 'Love Me Do' and 'She Loves You'."

"God, you really do take this band seriously, don't you?"

He glared at me. "Please don't take the Lord's name in vain."

I turned away, deciding that it wasn't worth trying to talk to him any further. I wasn't sure which thing I was more confused by, the fact that a Cillas fan apparently didn't like any of the Cillas' hits, or the way that everyone in the room seemed to be insistent on comparing this minor glam rock band to the Beatles. Still, this was only the very start of the tour, and I supposed I'd have plenty of time over the next few weeks to figure out what was behind all the strangeness I'd already encountered with this bizarre band.

Once the unpleasantness between Kate and Janine had finished, the rest of the rehearsal actually went smoothly, and eight hours later, when the working day finished, the room stank of mansweat and to-bacco smoke, but the musicians who had seemed so incompetent at the start had managed to pull together quite a professional-sounding half hour set, thanks more to Andy, Simon, and Jane, who had been working on their parts together for months, than to any of the old men who'd come in and added rudimentary parts on top.

At the end of the day, Andy gathered the musicians (other than Graham, who'd already left) round him.

"I'm proud of you all," he said. "We've still got a lot of work to do before the tour proper, but I think we've got a set here that will sound good for the showcase tomorrow. Look out world, the Cillas are back!"

# Bye Bye, Baby

I don't know if you've ever been to the Mermaid in London, but it's the kind of uber-corporate clean space that just screams "middle-management conference venue". It's also, appropriately enough, the place where Radio 2 put on their live shows, presumably because their target audience will all know where it is from having attended sales events there.

I'd never been to a gig there before – I don't tend to go to many gigs anyway, but the ones I go to tend to be in places which have some sort of character, and which aren't just big characterless spaces that feel like an open-plan office. But, you know, that was the job, and so it was off to the Mermaid to see a glam rock band who were big when my parents were half my age.

Surprisingly, I wasn't the youngest person there. I'd been expecting it to be grab-a-granny night, and indeed there were an awful lot of pensioners there, all glammed up for their one gig a year, but there were also at least a handful of teenage girls and younger women in the audience, and all looking genuinely excited and in gangs together, not like they'd been taken by their grandparents.

I decided that I wouldn't be doing my job as a journalist if I didn't at least try to find out what was going on there, so I went up to a couple of the younger-looking ones, who had purple hair and were wearing dresses that would barely have been a headband for me, and introduced myself.

It turned out that one of the girls, who introduced herself as Beth Harper, had read the book I'd written about the killings in April, and so she recognised my name, and the girls were instantly willing to talk about their fandom for the band.

"So is this some sort of ironic thing?" I asked. "Like are you just taking the piss out of these old people?"

"Not at all! We genuinely, absolutely, love this band. You don't spend all day redialling Radio 2 to try to get tickets for something just to take the piss out of it."

"Really? I mean, I don't want to seem rude, but..."

"Oh, don't worry, we've heard it all before. The Cillas were never the coolest band in the world, even when they were together, and it's mostly boring old men who like them now."

"So how come you like them then? I mean, I really don't want to..."

"No, it's fine, honestly. It's because of their TV show."

"TV show?"

"You don't know about that?" asked Beth's friend Claire. "They had their own TV series in the early 70s. A sort of variety thing, but it had a plot – loose sketches linked together into a story with songs, and they'd bring in Lulu or someone to do a song as well."

"So if it was in the 70s, how did you come to watch it?"

"There was this TV channel back in the day – PopUK, do you remember it? Anyway, they used to have it on in the evenings, as a sort of ironic rerun thing. A load of us used to watch it when we were little. It was dead funny, actually."

"Yeah," continued Beth, "and so a few years back I found a few of the old episodes up on YouTube, and I loved them, and started an Instagram about the band. I have like five thousand followers on there now, and we all talk about the Cillas, share gifs, that sort of thing."

"It's totes amazeballs," said Claire. I raised an eyebrow. "Okay," she admitted, "you're right, absolutely no-one says totes amazeballs in real life. I was fucking with you a bit, seeing if you're the kind of journalist who thinks we actually talk like that."

"Or you'll call us millennials," said Beth. "Millennials are all nearly forty now, but old people somehow seem to think that we're the same as them."

"Yeah, we're... generation Cilla!"

"No," said Beth, "we're really, really, not."

"I was fucking with her again, Beth."

"I could tell," I said, smiling.

"Hardly be worth fucking with you if you didn't know we were doing it, would it?" Beth had a point.

I thought that these girls would be perfect contacts for me to pump for background information on the band, and certainly they were far more on my wavelength than Chuck had been, and I decided I was going to have to get their contact details. Right then, though, I needed a piss, and I stood up to go off to the toilets.

Almost as if it was deliberately designed to frustrate me, though, that was the precise moment that the house lights dimmed and the intro music started up as Simon, Andy, and Jane took their places on the stage. I sat down, and hoped my bladder would forgive me.

I gave Jane a little wave, but she didn't wave back – I wasn't sure if that was because she'd not seen me, or because she was being all professional, but I didn't mind. I was surprisingly excited for the show.

So I sat there, uncomfortable from the pressure on my bladder, but getting into the show, and watched Simon, Andy, and Jane playing the riff for "Misty Lady ", as one at a time Sid, Pete, and Terry came on, plugged their instruments in, and started playing along. Then Graham came on, grabbed his mic, and started howling the lyrics as the crowd roared.

The venue was getting surprisingly hot and uncomfortable, and I wasn't sure whether it was because of the choking mists of dry ice coming from the stage or some fault in the air conditioning, but I was feeling distinctly sticky and unpleasant. I could see a number of the people in the audience were starting to sweat, and I couldn't imagine how intolerable it must have been for the band members on stage under those baking, searing, stage lights.

Certainly Graham seemed to be suffering – he mopped his fore-head several times during the guitar solos, and seemed almost to be choking on the high note at the end of the song, where he was meant to stretch out the "eeee" in "lady" for a good ten seconds without ac-companiment. His face was flushed, and I wasn't sure whether tears were coming out of his eyes, or if it was just sweat dripping down his face.

But I'll say this for Graham – he was a trouper, and he got through the long high note and through the song itself. At the end he raised both his arms, in what I'm sure was meant to be a look of triumph, but with the strain on his face it seemed more like a surrender.

"Good evening London!" he shouted hoarsely. "We're the Cillas! Did you miss us?!" The roar from the crowd suggested that they had indeed desperately missed the Cillas, and it also gave the red-looking singer a chance to catch his breath for a second.

"Blimey, it's hot in here, innit?" He said, and got a brief burst of polite nervous laughter from the crowd. He bent down and picked up a bottle of mineral water near his mic, then held it up in the air towards the crowd. "I'm betting whoever's in charge of the heating here has shares in Evian, because I'm going to get through about seventy of these things tonight, I think."

This time the laughter was more genuine. He grinned, his face still flushed. "Cheers!" He raised the bottle to his mouth and downed it in one. He threw the empty bottle to the side of the stage, where a roadie quickly scuttled over and collected it.

"This next one is..." He paused. "Fuck. I feel... shit..."

His face turned even redder, and he started gasping for breath and dropped to his knees. Pete shouted from behind his drum kit "Shit! He's having a heart attack!" and Andy – who had been in the process of changing guitars and was temporarily unencumbered, ran over to the centre of the stage and started feeling Graham's face. He picked up the mic, which Graham had dropped, and said "Is there a doctor in the audience? This is an emergency. This is not part of the show ", before turning back to Graham and attempting CPR on him.

No doctors came forward. After a few seconds, Andy grabbed the mic again. "I'm panicking here, I'm losing the rhythm. Can you give me a one twenty bpm click in my ear?" He was presumably talking to the sound engineer, and a second later I saw him pressing his hand to his left ear, where his in-ear monitor was, and then he started again, trying to compress Graham's chest.

The crowd was in uproar, with everyone panicking. Some were trying to grab video of the moment on their phone – either the same arseholes who slow down to look at car crashes or just people who, despite everything, didn't believe this was anything other than a rather tasteless bit of stagecraft – while others were crying. At least one bloke in the front row seemed to pass out himself.

Andy continued attempting to force air into Graham's lungs and restart his heart for what seemed like an eternity, though in reality it was probably no more than ten minutes before paramedics arrived and took over. They took Graham away on a stretcher, but it was very obvious to everyone there that he was already dead, and had probably died before Andy even got to him.

The show was over. And so, it seemed, were the Cillas.

# She'll Be Crying Over You

The next few hours were the kind of confusion you normally only see in the aftermath of major terrorist attacks. Half the people backstage were in floods of tears (and not necessarily the ones you'd expect – Terry of all people was practically screaming in grief, despite how Graham had treated him) and all the rest were on mobile phones.

While Graham had demanded that the rehearsal room and dressing rooms be alcohol-free, he hadn't been able to make any such demands of the venue bars, and so everyone backstage very quickly got very drunk indeed on the overpriced whisky and brandy. Some of the bar staff had made a bit of a fuss about being expected to work after the show had finished, but management had quickly pointed out to them that these were exceptional circumstances, and that the band and crew definitely needed drinks.

I wandered through the backstage area in something of a daze, looking for Jane. It was a weird experience – half of the conversations I overheard were the normal kind you'd hear in the immediate aftermath of a sudden death –"he was too young to go like that ", "does his wife know?", "has he got any children who need contacting?" – but the other half seemed to be far more focused on cancelling rehearsal studios and setting up press conferences. Death is apparently big business in the rock industry.

I tried to stay out of it, other than comforting Jane, who'd never seen anyone die before, and was completely broken up. She'd worked with Graham longer than half the people here, although they'd never been close, and so she was understandably in shock. I held her tight and told her it was going to be okay.

It wasn't, of course – there was no way the tour could go on, which meant she wasn't going to be earning any money for the next couple of months unless she could pick up a few quick, less lucrative, jobs. And that meant that our rent was fucked for starters. But all that was stuff we'd have to deal with later. The important thing here was that a man had died.

But whether it was going to be okay or not, I needed to let Jane know I was there for her. I also needed to figure out what this meant for our finances, but the important thing here was to make my wife feel better. We both knew that talk about money could wait at least until the poor bloke's corpse was cold.

But while Jane and I saw it that way, Graham's "old friends" apparently didn't.

"What the fuck are we going to do?" asked Sid. "We were meant to be starting the tour next week, and now we've got no fucking lead singer."

"We'll have to cancel. No other option," Terry replied. "It's not like we've got much choice in the matter."

"Fuck!" Pete said. "Fuck fuck fuck *fuck fuck*! I've got thirty grand in credit card debt I need to pay off! Where am I going to get that now?"

"You could do the autograph shows, Pete."

"Oh yeah, I can definitely see that working. 'pay for an autograph from the bloke who was the drummer in that band, but not the one who played on their biggest hit'. I'll be lucky if I get thirty p, let alone thirty thousand pounds."

"Better start looking into bankruptcy law then," said Sid.

"Oh, *very* helpful. Thank you *so much* for your support."

*At least you're not actually dead*, I thought to myself, but I didn't say anything. After all, they'd known Graham nearly fifty years. If they didn't like him, that probably said a lot in itself.

Anyway, Jane was still sobbing into my shoulder. I stroked her hair, which was getting longer than she normally wears it, and thought about how much death both of us had seen that year. Still, at least we were alive, and that was something.

And then, of all people, Kate Michaels walked into the room. All eyes immediately turned to her, and I began to cringe, wondering what fireworks might happen now.

At first, I couldn't imagine what Kate could be doing there. There was no way she was there to speak with the band, or to commiserate with Janine – they clearly hated each other, and I couldn't imagine that Kate was so lacking in social skills that she'd impose on a grieving widow within an hour or two of her husband's death.

As it turned out. she headed over to the band members, who were busy drinking themselves into a stupor with what was left of the drinks the promoter had obtained for them, making the most of it since they wouldn't have another chance at free backstage booze in the foreseeable future.

"Ey up, Kate," said Sid. "Fucking shit about Graham, innit?"

She looked appropriately respectful. "It's awful. I hope one of you will pass on my condolences to Janine. I would talk to her myself, but... you know."

The band members all nodded.

"Fancy a drink?" said Pete. "Might as well get plastered – it's not like they'll be asking us for an encore."

No-one laughed.

"Actually," she said, "I've come to offer you all a business proposition."

"I may be hard up," said Terry, "but not so hard up I need you to proposition me, and anyway I know your husband. Oh, what the hell, okay, I'll do it, but I have to keep me socks on."

The other band members laughed, dutifully, while Kate looked slightly queasy. I knew how she felt – shock and grief make people say odd things sometimes, but still.

Kate somehow managed to avoid actually vomiting, and said "If I could be serious for a moment... Robert's said that in the circumstances he might consider joining the tour as lead singer."

The band looked utterly flabbergasted. They seemed to take this news far less calmly than they'd taken their colleague's death. Pete actually choked on his whisky, and if Andy hadn't gone over to him and slapped him on the back, hard, I'm not at all sure that there wouldn't have been a second death in the band that night.

I knew nothing about Robert except that he'd been in the band in the past, that he hadn't joined them on this tour, and that he still had some sort of say in the band's business, but the reactions made it clear that Robert Michaels returning to the band was somewhere in between the second coming of Christ and getting a white man on Twitter to acknowledge that a woman has made a valid point, in terms of improbable events.

"What? You've got to be fucking kidding," said Terry. "He hasn't played live in decades."

"Well, neither have you," Kate pointed out.

"But.. I mean, we asked him when we were putting the show together. He said no."

"And now he's saying yes," said Kate. "At least for the moment. We can see what happens after this tour, but he's in for now."

"I say we go for it," said Terry. "We need one of Robert or Graham there – they're the only two who were on every Cillas album, they were the voices of the band. If you're going to have a Cillas tour you need at least one of them. And if we don't have a Cillas tour then we all lose a fuckload of money."

"We could do it without him," said Pete. "Andy can sing his parts well enough – he's been doing it in rehearsal anyway. There's still three of us, and there are plenty of bands our age that go out there with less members than that. Most of the audience won't even know who's who anyway. We could send the bloody Sweet out in our place and maybe three people would know the difference. We've no need to cut him in."

"Bollocks," said Sid. "Everyone knew who Graham was."

"Yeah," said Pete. "But Graham was Graham. He had solo hits, he had a career. We needed him. But we don't need Robert."

"You do," said Kate, "and you know very well why. If you want to go on tour as Sid, Pete, and Terry, that's one thing, but if you want to go out as the Cillas you need Robert and Graham... well, Janine now, I suppose, to let you use the name. And we're not doing that without Robert being there, on stage."

"Wait a second," said Sid, "he was absolutely determined not to join us on this tour, and now all of a sudden he's saying we can't do it without him? What the hell is going on here?"

"He has his reasons, and I'm sure he'll explain them to you in time," said Kate. "But for right now, he's going to be on this tour, or there's going to be no tour."

The band members looked at each other, and came to an agreement without having to speak.

"Okay," said Pete. "Looks like we've got no choice."

Kate smiled. "Thank me later, boys, your prodigal genius has re-turned."

# Get Down and Get With It

While they'd agreed to let Robert rejoin the band, there was still a lot to discuss. The band members had become a lot more serious in their demeanour in the last few minutes, and they seemed even to be sobering up. They retreated, along with Kate, to a corner of the dressing room, to discuss their sudden change in plans

"How is this actually going to work, though?" Pete asked. "I mean, this is Robert we're talking about. The man's a legendary recluse. He makes Greta Garbo seem like bloody James Corden. He stopped making music back in the seventies."

"So did we, to be fair," replied Terry.

"Yeah, but Sid's been doing session work. And I've kept my hand in. And I know the parts backwards. Even when he was actually playing, Robert could barely remember the chords to half the songs."

"He doesn't really need to remember the chords, though," said Sid. "He was only playing rhythm anyway, and half the songs he was just doubling the riffs Ray played. Stick my guitar through a signal splitter, add a bit of delay on one channel, it'll sound the same as two people playing. And anything where he was playing a separate part, Andy'll cover it like he has been anyway. He only needs to hold the guitar. It's his voice we need."

Pete thought about it for a few seconds. "I don't like it. You all know that I have no time at all for the man. He's an arse of the first order, and I can't imagine what it would be like having to work with him again for two months."

"Do you like it more or less than you like the idea of losing your house to pay that thirty grand of credit card debt?" Sid asked.

37

"You have a very good point, and I for one welcome our new Robert... no, I can't even say it. Look, I know we're desperate, but do we really want to tour with that fucker?"

"If we do, we'll make enough cash to retire on. And if we don't, there's a good case that we could be liable for all the costs of the tour so far. I'm not exactly Robert's biggest fan either, but it's not like we'd have to spend any time with him. Turn up to the gigs, separate dressing rooms, go out there 'hello Croydon', play for a couple of hours, off on opposite sides of the stage. You'd literally never even have to speak to him."

Terry chipped in. "Look, I'll say what we're all thinking. Frankly, they don't legally need any of us to do it at this point. Robert could go out there with a bunch of session players and call himself the Cillas, so we don't have a leg to stand on. And I don't know about you two, but I've not exactly had job offers pouring in these last forty years."

The other two nodded, slowly.

"Is there any reason – other than that none of us like the man – not to let him come on the tour? Can he still sing?"

Kate had been quiet during all of this – surprisingly so, given the way she had been fighting her absent husband's case in the re-hearsals. She clearly expected his old colleagues to detest him as much as they apparently did, and was wisely not trying to argue with them. But at this point she chipped in. "I can answer that," she said. "Here's something he's been working on."

She pulled out her phone, and tapped the screen a few times. Music came out. It wasn't very good – very slick, eighties-sounding, bland pop – but the voice on it was recognisably that of Robert Michaels, the man who'd sung the high harmonies and second lead on almost all the Cillas' hits. It sounded like a Cillas record. A remarkably shit one, mind you, but that was what it sounded like. Until I heard it, I hadn't realised how much Michaels' voice was missing from the live band.

The others listened carefully.

"What... what is this?" Pete asked. "That's... what's going on?"

"We've been in discussions for a while," said Kate, "and we weren't going to talk about this with you until some more details have been firmed up, but we've been preparing to make a new Cillas record, with Robert's new songs. We were going to tell you in a week or two. That's one of Robert's demos."

Sid scratched his chin and looked thoughtful. "It sounds okay, actually" he said, eventually.

"And is that a proper take?" Terry asked, "it's not some comped-together processed thing from fifty different takes?"

Kate laughed. "You know Robert. Can you really imagine him working that hard on anything?"

"That's a very good point," Pete said. "A very good point indeed. I never knew him to do a second take the entire time we were in the band. Okay, that settles it, he can still sing. But what's all this about a new album?"

"We weren't going to bring the idea to you until we'd got complete buy-in from the record label. But a little while ago Robert started writing again..."

"He what?" asked Pete.

"I know. He's not written anything in forty years, but he got together with a producer from LA, Jeff Washington, and they've been throwing ideas around. Jeff produced Graham's last solo record, and when he suggested making a new Cillas album, Graham put him in touch with me, and I got him together with Robert. The idea was that Robert would work with Jeff in the studio while the rest of you did the reunion tour, and then we'd get an album out."

"And what if we'd not agreed to work on this new album?" Pete asked.

Kate looked surprised. "That had honestly not occurred to any of us. None of you have done an album in forty years. You all need the money."

"She's got a point," said Terry.

"So anyway," Kate continued, "Robert hasn't been as absent from music as you thought. And while he didn't want to work with Graham any more – Jeff was going to produce his bits in the studio so Robert wouldn't have to be in the same room as him – now Graham's gone he's willing to do the tour."

The conversation was starting to bore me now, and I yawned and looked at my phone to see what time it was – it was gone midnight, it turned out – but I could tell that the band members were suddenly a lot more interested. Not only did Robert actually still sound good – in fact, to my ears, he sounded rather better than Graham had – there was the possibility of a new album to go with the tour. Jane's told me enough about musicians of that generation that I know that even though touring is where the money is, they see recording as being what makes someone a legitimate musician. The chance to get into the studio again was something that could get them to agree to a lot of things they would otherwise have had nothing to do with.

While this was going on, Jane had been looking down at her phone. She pulled me over and showed me Chuck's fan site. "Seen this? He's already got the news of Graham's death on there, the fucking vulture."

I had a look. She was looking at a website that was clearly done as a homebrew HTML thing rather than using a CMS – all black text on a salmon-pink background, with low-resolution jpegs for navigation. It was an antique throwback to the days of Geocities, and I realised that even though Chuck was only a few years older than me he'd clearly got online in 1997 or so and not bothered to update his web skills since. But while his web design skills were stuck in the Clinton era, you couldn't fault the content for not being on the bleeding edge.

Chuck had already updated his site, with photos of Graham's body being taken out of the venue, and with a review of the one song they'd performed (he'd said it was a mediocre effort, and criticised Jane's keyboard parts as sounding plasticy and eighties, which made me fume). He didn't seem to think that the lead singer having died was a reason to grade on a curve, and his report of the death seemed utterly unconnected from his review of the gig.

And as for his take on the death... well, I'm not one to talk about not speaking ill of the dead, but even I wouldn't say anything like "let us hope that in his final moments he repented of his heretical beliefs, in order to avoid the hellfire to which his perversion of Christianity would otherwise have doomed him."

I scrolled down a bit, and saw something else, which made me even angrier. The entire previous post on his site was copied, without attribution, from the dummy placeholder text I'd written for the first draft of the tour booklet. I was going to have words with that man. Stealing my work while putting down my wife's playing? That came close to a death sentence in my book.

And then I remembered what had just happened, and realised that "death sentence" might not be the most appropriate thing to be thinking.

But Chuck Bentley had made my shit list, and before this tour was over I wanted my revenge.

# Gudbuy t'Jane

When Jane and I got back to the hotel room where we were staying, it was almost three AM. I wanted to go to sleep right then, but Jane just sat and stared. Something was bothering her, something other than Graham's death. I made her a cup of herbal tea, using the little kettle on the bedside table, and she took it from me and smiled, but said nothing.

We sat for a while on the bed, as our hotel room wasn't big enough to have chairs – a clinically-white bedspread on a double bed, a carpet in that green colour they have in hotels that doesn't show vomit too badly, a television bolted to the wall, and a single bedside table took up all the room in the bedroom, so if you wanted to sit down you had a choice of the bed or the toilet in the "*en suite* bathroom" (which was effectively just a door blocking off a corner of the room with a shower in it).

Jane wasn't talking, but I knew she needed to get something off her chest, so eventually I asked her. "What's the matter love? I know it's not just Graham. There's something else, too, isn't there?"

"No, there's nothing. Go to sleep."

That's not like her – it's usually me who's crap at emotional communication, while she's able to get her feelings across in what some might say was rather too much detail at times, at least if it was them who'd pissed her off.

"Come on. You can tell me. It's something about money, isn't it? You never get like this over anything else. What's up?"

"What do you think?"

I thought for a second. "It's something to do with the tour, isn't it?"

She nodded, and started crying. She never cries, but when her role as provider was threatened, that must have seemed like an attack on her very existence – she thinks that's the only thing she's good for, no matter how often I tell her I love her for everything else she is. I held her as tight as I could, trying to squeeze all the tension out of her, though I could feel her muscles as solid as rocks. I started to kiss the tears away, but she shook her head. I knew that shake – it's the one she does when she thinks she doesn't deserve to be comforted.

I couldn't explain to her that it wasn't even about what she deserved, but about what I needed. I needed her to feel well, so I could cope myself. I needed her happiness more than my own.

"But sweetheart," I said, "the tour's not being cancelled! It's going ahead!"

"That doesn't matter," she said. "What use is that to me? If Robert's coming back, they won't need me."

"What do you mean, they won't need you?"

She sighed. "Robert Michaels was the rhythm guitarist, yes, but he also played all the keyboard parts on the records, and used to play piano live. Why would they need me, when they've got the bloke who played those parts right there?"

I could see her point.

"I'm useless. I'm a useless waste, I barely make enough for us to live on, and now I'm not even going to make that!"

There, I couldn't see her point at all. How could I convince her that none of this was her fault, that she was an innocent victim in all this, and that we would be fine financially with or without her tour income? Fucking late capitalism, causing us to value ourselves only by our labour value.

(Yes, I do think that kind of thing even when I'm trying to comfort my crying wife. The perils of spending too much time on politics Twitter. I now think entirely in soundbite slogans and memes.)

I just held her, the salt taste of her tears still on my lips, the smell of her hair in my nostrils, while she let it all out – all the frustration of being the only woman in a gang of men, the fear of having to cope without her income, all of it.

It took a long time for her breathing to calm down.

"Maybe we'll be okay," she eventually said. "After all, I have a contract. They can't just sack me without paying me off, not if the tour's going to continue. I won't get the full amount, of course, but I'll get something, and that'll probably be enough to cover the mortgage. We'll have a bit of a shit Christmas, of course, but I think we can probably manage."

I smiled. I needed her to feel better, and this was a good start, although I was going to have to spend a lot more time helping her get over this.

Just then, a knock came from our door.

"Who the hell can that be?" I muttered. "We didn't order room service, and it's not like we were making that much noise." I assumed it was someone at the wrong door, and was prepared to give them the bollocking of a lifetime for bothering us at that hour of the night, but when I opened it I was surprised to see Pete, the Cillas' drummer. He looked even greyer than normal – Graham's death seemed to have shocked him enough that he'd gone right past his normal John Major look and all the way into Romero zombie territory.

"What's up?" I asked. "You okay?"

"Can I come in? I know it's late, but I heard you talking as I was going past to my own room."

I was about to tell him that no, he couldn't come in at half past bloody three in the morning, but Jane called out "sure, come on and join us." I knew what that tone of voice meant – it meant that under no circumstances did she want to continue our conversation, and that she welcomed the distraction, and so I grudgingly let him in.

"Sit down," said Jane, patting the bed next to her.

"So I'm getting into bed with two lesbians, eh?" He smirked, and I felt like punching him, but Jane let out the kind of fake laugh that means "you are a man in a position of financial power over me, and if I am going to get my payoff for this tour I'll need to keep on your right side, so I'll pretend to find you funny even though had anyone else said that I'd have removed his scrotum."

It's amazing how much she can communicate with a laugh. And how oblivious to everything she's communicating men can be. Why even *are* men?

"So what is it you want?" I asked, trying not to sound too aggressive. "Just need someone to talk to?"

"Not quite. I'm here to talk to Jane, actually. I've come to tell you we'll still be needing you for the tour."

Jane boggled. "But surely Robert..."

"Look, I'll be frank. The others weren't entirely sure if we needed another keyboard player now that Mr Robert Bloody Genius is swanning in and saving us all. But I told them straight – we need Andy and Simon to cover for us, and we at least used to be competent at playing our own instruments. Robert was a lazy arse who never practised. We'll be lucky if he even remembers the difference between the black and white keys. He was a shit player, and you're great. We need you."

Jane smiled through the tears. "He wasn't that bad. Some of the playing on *Goodbye Dragon* is..."

"Yeah, well, you can fix a lot of bum notes if you spend long enough in the studio. You should have heard him when we tried to tour that album. Fucking embarrassment. Thank God the sound systems were so bad in those days that no bugger could hear what he was playing. Look, you're all right, love. You've still got the job. Just keep playing the same parts you were, and if he's so great he can play round them."

"Really? This is amazing!"

"Yeah," Pete said. "Bit of a bloody emotional roller-coaster today, isn't it? Half me muscles are spasming and I feel like I'm going to throw up. I've had more emotional highs and lows in the last couple of hours than I had in my whole forties. I'm going to head back off to my own room before someone comes in and tells me my son's been run over but he left me his winning lottery ticket or something. See you in rehearsal tomorrow."

He got up, and I smiled at Jane as he walked out and closed the door behind him. "See? I told you it was all going to be okay, didn't I?"

She shook her head. "It's not all okay. We've got money, but Graham's still dead. I'm not sure if I even want to be doing this any more."

"Look, you know, if you want to quit..."

"No. No, I'm not going to quit. But I think Pete had the right idea. I think we should head off to bed."

"I agree. Tonight has been an utter disaster, but we've got a free hotel bed, and we should make the most of it."

I thought I wouldn't sleep, being so wound up after seeing Graham die and Jane so upset. But it was so late, and I'd been held together with adrenaline that finally stopped coursing through my veins after Pete left. I think I was asleep before my head hit the pillow.

# King of the Mountain Cometh

At rehearsal the next day, everyone was on edge, as you might expect given the unusual circumstances. The musicians sat around in a circle for a quick meeting, while Chuck and myself sat to one side observing them.

I glared at Chuck, trying to send the telepathic message that he was in big trouble for nicking my material, but he seemed oblivious.

Pete was nervously drumming on his own legs with his sticks, Sid was nervously puffing on a roll-up that was even skinnier than him, and Terry wasn't actually looking at anyone, but looking down at his own fingers as he ran through the parts he was still unsure of on his unplugged bass. Simon was crouched on his chair, folded up on himself in the way no-one over twenty-five can do without spending the next two hours unstiffening themselves, and Jane... Jane was her normal Janey self. Andy seemed the most shaken, but he was also still the consummate professional, and as musical director he was in charge.

"Okay, so Robert's going to be turning up in an hour or two, so we've got time to work out what the new setlist should be, and get a bit of work done on the new running order and routines. Obviously Janine's dance section's going to be dropped," a sarcastic round of applause there from Sid and Pete, "but most of the rest of it Robert can cover just as well as Graham. I've been listening to his demos, and his top end's gone a little, but he was always the high harmony singer so he can probably cover Graham's range without any major changes. The main thing is his instrumental parts..."

The three older men laughed.

"What's funny?"

"He won't be playing any parts," said Pete. "Not if he's the same old lazy bastard Bob he always was."

"But didn't he play guitar and keyboards?"

"Sort of," said Sid, "but we used to give him these little two-note riffs and stuff to play and keep him low in the mix."

"So we just give him a guitar as a prop and have him do just the vocals?" Andy asked. The others nodded. "Okay, that makes things much easier. Do any of you have anything else you'd like us to do differently, now we're having to shake things up?"

"Well, we'll have to change all the video screen stuff," said Pete.

"Already on it," said Andy. "We should have new videos sorted by the time of the next show. Anything else?"

"Well I was thinking," said Sid, "should we perhaps have some sort of tribute to Graham, where we play along with one of his vocal tracks or something?"

"Isn't that a bit tacky?" Pete replied.

"I dunno, I quite like it," Terry said.

"It's a bit early for that sort of thing, though, isn't it?" Pete said. "He's not even been buried yet, so playing with his vocal track would just seem weird."

"Tell you what," said Andy, "playing an instrumental track to a pre-existing vocal is a ballache anyway, and the technical stuff fails half the time. How about before the interval we have a bit where we say 'blah blah sad loss, can never be replaced, show in memory of him et cetera', then play one of his solo videos at the start of the intermission, after we've all got off stage?"

"That could work," said Pete.

"Yeah, I could go for that," said Sid. "Yeah, do that. Use 'Heaven's Here'. It's a godawful track, but... you know, heaven."

"Okay," said Andy, scribbling notes on a scrap of paper. "Anything else we need to talk about? No? Okay, let's get started."

The band went to their instruments, spent a few minutes twiddling and tuning up, and then began a run-through of "Rich Girl Blues", with Andy taking the lead vocal.

"Oy oy!" A voice came from the door. "Someone trying to take my job are they? That's a demarcation issue! I'll have the union on you!" Robert Michaels had arrived.

I don't know what you expect when you're thinking about a reclusive musical genius who's barely left his house in forty years, but I imagine you think of someone with a beard down to his waist, maybe with four-foot-long toenails and eyes that point in two different directions. Certainly that was what I was expecting from the Cillas' own example of the White Man Who Took Too Many Drugs For This World.

But as it turns out, my first thought when looking at Robert Michaels, as he entered the room along with Kate, was "he doesn't look like a musical genius. He looks more like a retired car salesman dressed up for a Rotarian club dinner". He had thick white hair, vaguely swept back, and was wearing tinted glasses, white trousers, and a blue double-breasted blazer which he'd buttoned up. I half expected him to shake my hand and ask if he could count on my vote for him as Conservative candidate for my local council.

Terry and Sid immediately stood up, almost instinctively, and everything about their body language showed they thought of him as the boss. Both exclaimed "Robert!" and made general noises about how astonishingly good it was to see him, which he acknowledged with the slightest nod of the head.

Pete, on the other hand, didn't even look up from his kit. He was ostentatiously ignoring Robert, as if he didn't want to acknowledge his existence.

"All right there, Pete?" Robert called from the doorway. Pete muttered something that could have been "yeah" or could have been significantly ruder, and then continued his discussion with Andy about the drum fill for "Rich Girl Blues." While Sid and Terry had been largely content with just getting through their parts adequately, and trusting the backing players to keep everything together, Pete had been increasingly getting into the rehearsals, and I was starting to wonder if they even needed Simon there at all any more. And then I felt guilty – I was thinking the same about Simon that Jane had been thinking about herself. He needed the job too.

Robert stepped to the mic stand in the centre of the room and said, "Okay, the Cillas, together again for the first time!"

"Apart from the last few weeks," muttered Pete to himself, but if Robert heard he pretended not to.

Kate came over and sat with me and Chuck.

"This should be a bit easier now Janine's not here," she said.

"Of course, you'll still have to get her approval for everything you're doing, won't you?" Chuck said.

Kate glared at him. "Yes, we will, but she's not here. Of course, it's awful what happened to Graham, and no-one could have wished for that, but... it makes things easier."

She was all heart, clearly. I took a hopefully-casual-looking step away to let her and Chuck talk to each other. They deserved each other. I was going to ignore them and concentrate on what the band were doing.

Robert had taken Graham's old place at the mic stand. "Okay," he said, "let's start with 'She's My Lady'."

"Actually," said Andy, "we've already got that one down pretty well. If you know the part, there are things we need to rehearse more urgently. Let's try 'For All We Know' shall we?"

Robert looked mildly annoyed at having his leadership role usurped by a hired hand, but he nodded.

"What key are we in again on this one, Andy?" asked Phil.

"That's a point." Andy turned to Robert. "The original of this one was in E, but we dropped it down to D because Graham had lost some range on the top end. Are you going to be more comfortable singing it in D or in E?"

"I don't really give a shit, mate. Have you got a lyric sheet?"

I was quite surprised that Robert didn't know the words to one of his own biggest hits, but Andy just nodded and went and rummaged in a pile.

"Here we go. We were using iPads but a couple of the guys found them hard to work with. We'll have a teleprompter on stage for the shows themselves, if remembering lyrics is going to be a problem. Do you want a chord chart or just the lyrics?"

"Better just give me the words for now. One thing at a time, eh? I'll get the guitar part sorted later."

"Keyboard," Pete muttered.

"Eh?"

"You played keyboard on 'For All We Know'. When you weren't too pissed to find the keys, anyway. Ray played the only guitar on that one. Don't you remember?"

Pete's voice was sharp and bitter. He clearly resented having Robert here at all, and wasn't going to make any allowances for the elapsed time.

"You're quite right. Keyboard it is, mate." He stood at the mic, holding the mic stand in his right hand and clutching the lyric sheet at eye level in his left. "Shall we?"

"Okay, 'mate'," said Pete, the quote marks audible. "One two three four!"

Jane played the piano intro, Trevor and Andy strummed their guitars dramatically, and the rhythm section clattered in with their massive two-drum-kit sound. I sat back and listened, enthralled. The Cillas were together again, again.

# Editions of You

After a couple of hours, the rehearsal broke up for lunch. Robert and Kate apparently had a hotel room in the vicinity to which they were returning for an hour, to have a lie down and get some energy back. Chuck was going to stay in the rehearsal room and take photos of the equipment for his website. But the rest of us, being dead classy like, headed to a local Greggs which had a sit-down table section. The blokes mostly got sausage rolls and steak bakes. For myself, I compromised my veganism enough to have a spinach and ricotta bake, on the grounds that there was probably slightly less dead animal in that than in most of the other things there, this particular Greggs not having any salads that weren't full of cheese and egg.

We sat down and shoved grease and stodge in our mouths, and Pete eventually started talking about what had been on everyone's mind since Robert first volunteered to rejoin.

"But can we make a new album? Sid's the only one of us who's been in a studio for thirty years."

Terry looked at Pete as if he were mad. "Of course we can make a fucking new album. We can play live, can't we? And we're sounding pretty great. And in the studio you can do as many takes as you need to do."

"But none of us know anything about the technology they use nowadays, all that Protunes and autotune and god knows what else. It's not like going into Trident and sticking it down on an eight track any more. I mean, I play drums. Do they even record drums any more, or is it all done by someone on a computer?"

"Well, if it's done on a computer, that'll make your job easier, won't it? You can just sit around and get pissed while the rest of us work our bollocks off doing seventy-eight takes of everything."

"I just think we should think about what it is that we're going to be doing," Pete said. "A bad show is forgotten the next day, but a bad record will be around long after we're dead. We need to think about that."

I didn't have the heart to tell him that these days a bad gig will live forever on YouTube, while an official recording's shelf-life was limited to however long it stayed on Spotify's Release Radar. He was still thinking in twentieth-century terms, but he was at least trying to consider the realities of the modern world. I wondered if I'd be as clueless in thirty years' time. Almost certainly.

Sid chipped in. "Look, they're not just going to leave us in there with no-one who knows what they're doing, are they? There'll be an engineer, and probably a producer assigned by the label. They're not just going to say 'here you go, chaps, have half a million quid of our money and do what you like so long as you give us a tape of something at the end'. That's another way it's not like it was in our day – the record companies are run by professionals, not by coke dealers now."

"That's a shame," Terry replied. "I could do with a bit of a toot now, and I haven't had a dealer who knew where to get the good shit in thirty years."

"Might help you burn off some of that steak bake," Sid said, and pointed at Terry's paunch.

"We can't all be so skinny we disappear if you look at us side-on," said Terry. "Anyway, at least I don't dye my hair!"

"Only because you've got none left!"

Pete smiled. "Okay, you're probably right that they'll put someone in charge of the album – but is it really our album then?"

"Were they ever?" Sid asked. "The early ones were all Robert and Ray telling us what to do, and *Goodbye Dragon*, I didn't even hear that til the basic tracks were done."

Pete took his glasses off, breathed on them, and cleaned them on his T-shirt before putting them back on. "There's a difference. We were working as a band then. We don't even really know each other any more. We were on more or less the same page creatively back in the 70s – we all loved the same music, we were playing together every night. That's not the case any more. We might be playing at being a gang again, but we've not got that unity of purpose any more."

"That could be a good thing," said Terry. "Remember the Beatles *White Album*? They were barely in the same room as each other for five minutes when they were making that, and it's a fucking banger of an album."

"Apart from 'Revolution Number Nine'," said Sid.

"Fair point, fair point. And that's where this outside producer will come in, I presume. Stop any of us doing a Jazz Odyssey."

"Damn," said Pete. "I was looking forward to my three-hour drum solo. I suppose I'll just have to write some actual songs, instead."

"Do you write songs?" asked Sid, surprised. "I never knew that."

Pete looked uncomfortable. "Yeah, well, when you're in a band with those massive egos strutting around the place, you don't really get a chance to show off, do you? Maybe now there's only one narcissistic cockhole in the band the rest of us will get the chance to do our own things a bit."

I wondered if that would be what the record company wanted, but I kept my thoughts to myself.

"How about you, Sid?" Pete asked, "You been writing at all?"

"Nah," said Sid. "I never fancied meself as a songwriter. You know how it is – I like to play, not to think. I just like the physical feel of an axe in my hands, and don't want to be sitting down and analysing things – it'd ruin everything. Happy to play anything you bring in, though."

"And you, Terry?" Pete asked. "Do you write?"

Terry laughed. "Don't you remember 'Car Crazy'?"

Pete laughed as well. "Oh yeah, I'd forgotten that one. B-side to 'Misty Lady', wasn't it?"

"Yeah, they let me write that one, and sing it as well. After that experience, I don't think anyone ever wants to hear anything I write ever again."

"Still," Sid said, "we'll have Robert's songs, anyway. I just hope he's not lost his touch. Forty years is a long time. Although then again that probably means he's got forty years worth of unreleased demos shoved in his sock drawer."

"You have a separate drawer just for your socks?" Terry said. "Always knew you were a posh Southern bastard."

"Why, what do you have?" Sid replied.

"Me feet." Said Terry. "One pair on me feet, the other pair hung up on the radiator, drying."

The others looked at him open-mouthed. He laughed at them. "Ah! Gotcha! Jesus, you lot will believe anything at all about Northerners, won't you? We're not fucking animals you know."

"I'm off to the bog," Pete said. "Back in a minute."

When Pete had got up, Sid turned to me.

"Is it me, or is Pete acting a bit odd?"

"Well," I thought for a second. "I suppose it depends what you mean by odd. I mean, this isn't exactly a normal situation."

"Suppose you're right," he said, and took a bite of Pete's steak bake while Pete was away. "I mean, it's an odd collection of people. Me and Pete had never even met Tel til a couple of weeks ago, and now Robert's back after forty years."

"Hang on, what do you mean you'd never met Terry?"

"Ah," said Terry. "You didn't realise? I was never in the band with these two. It was my band originally, when we were still the Godzillas. But I was never the best player in the world, and after the first few hits, Graham and Robert got together with Clive the manager and decided they were going to sack me and Dave, the drummer, and get in some better players. They said that they needed a black bloke like Sid on bass because he'd have better rhythm."

Sid looked at him open mouthed. "They fucking never!"

"Swear down, that's what they said."

Sid shook his head. "I never knew that. You think you know people..."

"Course," Terry continued, "with Ray dead, now Sid's moved from bass to lead guitar, so I get me old job back."

"So it's not much of a reunion, then," I said. "Not if you all never played together."

"Suppose you're right," said Sid. "But on the other hand, we *were* all in the Cillas."

"And what about this Dave?" I asked, vaguely curious.

"Oh, last I heard he was working as a pork butcher in Melbourne," Terry replied. "I got a Christmas card from him in 1983. Not heard from him since."

Pete arrived back. "Not heard from who?"

"Oh, no-one," Terry looked vaguely guilty. "We were just talking about old friends and that."

Pete nodded. "Suppose we'd better get back to work," he said. "Let's rock and roll."

# The Ballroom Blitz

As it turned out, Graham's death hadn't even caused the band to have to reschedule the tour. I'd had to work my arse off writing press releases and rewriting the tour programmes, which they'd had to rush-produce (they sold the ones featuring Graham on eBay for triple the original asking price, and they got snapped up by a particularly ghoulish type of collector), but for the band themselves it seemed like it was almost just roll-on roll-off lead singers. Other than Pete's tetchiness with Robert, nothing had changed there, and the band were ready within a week for the start of the tour proper.

The opening night of the tour was at the Liverpool Empire. The Empire was by some way the smallest venue the tour was going to hit, but the idea had always been to start the tour off small and in the regions, so they'd be able to get road-seasoned before playing any of the bigger venues they were booked in later.

The Empire's quite a nice venue, though. It's intimate, but at least from the inside it still looks like a classy proper theatre, and the acoustics of the place are lovely. And the seats are comfortable, which was a relief, because I needed a rest. I'd got there by train and discovered it was quite a trek from Lime Street station, and uphill all the way. When you've got little legs like mine, that sort of walk can easily wear you out, and I sank into my seat determined that no matter how good the band were, I wasn't going to stand up for anything for at least an hour.

Jane, Simon and Andy walked out onto the dark stage while the intro tape was still playing, taking their places with their instruments. Jane was stood stage left behind a bank of keyboards (half of them just for show), Andy stage right with a single guitar (techs were backstage furiously tuning up half a dozen more for him to swap to during the course of the show), and Simon at a kit behind Jane, not on a riser like Pete's.

The house lights dimmed, and the audience started to roar, as the intro music (a compilation of glam hits that Andy had put together) faded and the strobe lights started up. A video montage of shots of the band members from their seventies heyday started up (carefully missing out shots of the old drummer, Dave, and edited to give the impression of the men on stage having all played with each other). Simon counted out the beats on a cymbal (for show rather than for any real reason – all three people on stage had clicks in their in-ear monitors) and then they started up the instantly-recognisable riff of "Goin' My Way."

Andy stepped up to the mic, still in darkness, and said "Ladies and gentlemen, welcome to the Cillas' fiftieth anniversary show! Together again for the first time, the original Cillas! Please welcome to the stage... Pete Le Mesurier!"

Pete walked onto the stage, waving and followed by a spotlight which did nothing to make him look any less grey. He made his way to the kit in the centre of the stage with the band's logo on the bass drum, and started playing fills, embellishing the part Simon was playing.

"Terry Pattison!"

Terry walked out from the other side of the stage, nodded to the crowd, picked up his bass, and joined in, immediately turning to the two drummers to make sure he was locked in with them. The lights reflected off his bald spot as he turned round, and I vaguely wondered if he'd polished it to get that effect.

"Sid Berry!"

Sid jumped onto the stage, struck a few karate poses, picked up his guitar, and started soloing immediately. A few of the women in the audience made "ooh" noises, as if overcome with lust, and I wasn't sure whether they intended it ironically or not. Whatever their intent, it made him grin.

"And ladies and gentlemen, the lead vocalist of the Cillas, back together after more than forty years – the genius himself; the one, the only, Mister ROBERT MICHAELS!"

The other band members rolled their eyes, but the audience wasn't paying attention to them as Robert shuffled hesitantly on to the stage, head bowed as if he didn't want to be there, picked up his guitar, and walked to the microphone and started strumming. And probably even fewer of them noticed Andy stepping on an extra pedal at the same moment Robert's strumming started – as far as they were concerned, Robert started playing, the sound got thicker, that must be his guitar. If they were thinking about it that much.

"Hello Liverpool, it's great to be back!" Robert shouted, before starting to sing. "I got a reason for believin' there's a trip to take today/You keep teasin', you ain't leavin', you've come back to stay – all together!"

And the crowd chorused "Little girl, are you goin' my way?"

I couldn't help but admire the way he had the crowd enraptured. The show that Graham had played with the band, the one where he'd died, he'd been adored by the audience, but he'd been a teen idol and half of them would have swooned no matter what he did, remembering him from the seventies. This was different. The crowd were willing him on. They knew from the tour publicity that Robert was a genius who hadn't played live in decades, and they would have forgiven anything at all from someone who seemed so broken.

He was singing really well, but I wasn't at all convinced he even knew where he was – I was getting really mixed messages from him in the rehearsals. Sometimes he could be sharp, in a used-car-salesman sleazy wide-boy sort of way, but then five minutes later he could seem completely unaware of the most basic aspects of the world around him. He could be incredibly lazy about learning his own parts, and the slightest thing going wrong could throw him completely. I wasn't at all sure he was well enough to be performing, but Chuck had been enraptured by "the genius" and had insisted to me that him being there would "make the fans cream."

The first half of the set went well – the band played impeccably, Jane looked gorgeous, and Robert was perfectly capable of reading the words off his teleprompter – but I wondered why the fans were so impressed with Robert. Handily, in the bar, I bumped into Claire and Beth, the fans I'd met at the London show.

After a bit of preliminary squeeing at seeing each other, I asked Claire what she thought of Robert.

"Ah, I wish Graham was here instead," she said, "but having him there is better than nothing, I suppose."

"I got the impression that the fans thought he was the most important member of the band," I said, mildly surprised.

She laughed. "Oh, some fans, yeah. The ones who like to make lists of what brand of amplifier they used on their 1972 tour and what kind of dust was on the mixing console in the studio where they made 'Misty Lady'."

"Yeah," Beth joined in, "the point-missing anal men who don't like the idea of the band being fun."

"I've never got those people at all," Claire said. "I mean, the whole point of the Cillas is to be fun. It's not like they're Radiohead or something."

At this, both women stuck their tongues out in mock disgust at the idea of Radiohead. I had to laugh.

"Yeah, it was Chuck Be..." I couldn't even finish the sentence before both of them interrupted simultaneously.

"Chuck Bentley?! He's the fucking worst" said Beth.

"Did he try to get you onto his podcast?" Claire asked.

"Oh, you know him then?"

"You could say that," said Claire, angrily. "He's the tosser who took all the stuff from my Tumblr and stuck it on his fan site without credit. I'd spent years collecting those issues of *Look-In* and *Lindy* and scanning the comic strips from them."

"There were Cillas *comics*?" I asked incredulously.

"Oh yeah," she replied. "Annuals, too, with comic strips in, though whoever drew the ones in the 1973 annual must have been sent the wrong photos, because I'm pretty sure Sid didn't have white skin and blue eyes, wear a spotted neckerchief, and have a giant hoop earring."

I agreed that that sounded rather unlikely. He may have changed quite a bit, but I didn't think he'd changed that much.

"Anyway," she continued, "He took all my scans – but not my great captions for them, which were half the point – and stuck them on his site without any credit at all."

"He did that to me, too!" I chipped in. "He took huge chunks of my writing and just stuck them up on his page without any credit."

"He's a prick," Beth said. "But he gets all the backstage passes because he licks the important arses."

"If you want backstage passes," I said, "I can get them for you easily."

"Oh, we've already got them," said Claire. "We can lick arses too. We just don't like it."

I was about to ask them whose arse they were licking, but then the bell rang for the start of the second half, and we went back into the venue.

# Man Who Speaks Evil

Backstage the band had a chance to calm down in their dressing room before the last obligation of the night, going out into the back-stage bar and shaking hands and chatting with the dozen or so professional liggers, fan club members, and local DJs who'd managed to get themselves backstage passes.

Despite the initial talk of them having separate dressing rooms, the decision had been made that at least this early in the tour, while they were all getting to know each other again, they'd share one, and me being nosy I managed to talk my way into it.

I don't know if you've ever been in a dressing room shared by four men in their sixties and seventies, after they've just come off stage after an hour and a half under hot spotlights. If you haven't, and want to know what it's like, don't change your socks for a month and then take them off in a sauna. The sweat hung thick on the air, almost choking me.

And these were men who were also unafraid of letting it all hang out. Well, not everything, thank the Godess, but they were getting changed from their stage shirts into civvies, and my vision was filled on all sides by wrinkled, flabby, old-man guts and grey body hair.

The show had, for the most part, gone fantastically well, and the audience had called for more encores than the band had songs, so they'd had to repeat "Goin' My Way" at the end of the show. But as always with musicians, it was the one part that hadn't gone so well that they all remembered.

The band had learned one of the songs from Robert's new demos, and had played it as the penultimate song of the main show, to give the more hardcore fans in the audience a bit of a treat. But when I say the band had learned it, one member had learned it rather less well than the others.

Terry, towelling himself under the armpits with his T-shirt, turned to Robert and asked "so what the fuck was that all about? How did you fuck up 'The Looking Glass' so badly? I mean, you only wrote it last week. How could you forget the tune? The words I understand, but the tune?"

"Oh don't start. You didn't even learn you could put your fingers on the frets to make different notes until our third gig."

"That was fifty fucking years ago, Robert. And you made me pay for that, didn't you? I'm talking about today. The fucking tune only has about three sodding notes in it total. Thank God Andy was there to cover for you, that's all I'm saying."

"Yes, he was. And that's what I'm paying him for. Remember that – it's me paying him. I've saved this fucking tour, none of you would have jobs without me, and I could do with a little fucking respect for it."

I thought about the way he'd been content to sit back and let the others work and collect money for the tour, and only took the job once he'd had literally no other option, but I didn't say anything – it wasn't for me to get involved in the band members' interpersonal beef.

Terry's posture changed utterly once Robert's tone turned aggressive, though, and he seemed to shrink and become even smaller than his normal five foot four.

"Look, I'm sorry if I seemed like I was being a bit of a dick," he said. "It's the adrenaline from being on stage. All I was trying to do was ask a genuine question – how did you forget the words to a tune we're still only just recording?"

"Because we're still only just recording it," said Robert. "I'm still working out details of the melody. I may change it at some point. I've got about five versions of the fucker going on in my brain right now, okay?"

Terry nodded, and Robert fell silent, as the others talked about the gig. He just sat and stared into space.

"So do you think we might be taking 'Misty' a fraction too slow?" Andy asked. "The audience didn't seem to be getting into it as much as I'd have hoped."

"Nah," said Sid. "Opening night crowd, innit? They're not here to hear the hits, they've heard them a million times already. You saw that crowd – they're the type who want to hear some song we played live once in 1972 that's only on an Argentinian bootleg or something. That's not the typical crowd. I guarantee that the second-night crowd will be all about the hits. We'll be getting mass exoduses to the bar every time we don't do anything in the top ten, and they'll whoop for the hits like they're having an orgasm."

"That seems... a suspiciously precise assessment," said Pete. "Not that I'm disagreeing necessarily, I'd just be interested in how you formed that opinion."

Sid smiled. "I sat in on a few dates on one of Graham's solo tours last year, when we first started talking about getting the band back together. Just came out for the encores, you know? Just to see if I could still do it. And that was exactly how it went down then."

"He's right," said Chuck, who'd somehow managed to get himself into the dressing room, even though I couldn't see a backstage pass. "First night is for the hardcore, second night is for the casuals. That's how it always goes."

"And how did the audience react to Sid on those shows?" Robert asked, sullenly.

Sid looked embarrassed. "They didn't really seem to notice I was there."

"I think that proves my point," Robert said, and then turned away from them again.

"Why are you such an *arse* all the time, Robert?" interjected Sid. "I mean, really. All this *prima donna* bullshit, what's all that about? You might have started believing your own publicity, but the fact is that ninety percent of those people out there don't even know your name, let alone that you're 'the genius of the Cillas'. They know who the band are, but if the three of us went out tomorrow without you no-one would even notice."

Robert turned on Sid. "You know full well, mate, that I'm the only reason this tour can go ahead. I wrote those fucking songs you're out there playing, and you weren't even in the band when we made half those records. I hired you in 1972, and you've got a job again now because of me, and don't you forget it."

He pulled a T-shirt on and stormed out of the door, leaving the other band members confused and disorientated. Should they go out and do the handshakes-and-smiles thing and put up with all the fans and VIPs asking where the only important member of the band was, or should they go running after him and potentially leave the fans in the lurch?

After a few seconds' discussion, Pete eventually said, "Look, we can tell them that Robert is simply too highly-strung and geniusey to be able to meet with mere mortals, or some shit like that. They'll buy it, because they all think he's a fragile little snowflake. At least this way they'll get to meet some of us."

"Do you think so?" Terry asked.

Pete thought for a moment. "Do I buggery," he finally said. "I'll go and have a word with the grumpy old sod. You lot run a flannel over your unmentionables while I'm gone, you stink like a fucking sewer and we need to be clean for the meet and greet." He buttoned up his shirt and headed for the door, but almost ran into Kate, who was coming in.

"Look, I'm sorry about Robert," she said as soon as she'd recovered from nearly having a John Major lookalike knock her over. "He's just stressed. He's gone to cool down for five minutes, but he's going to do the meet and greet and he'll be fine with the fans. He said to tell you he's sorry. It's just a stressful situation for him."

"Yes, well," said Pete, "it's stressful for all of us, isn't it? He should remember that we're meant to be a band, not a boss and his sidemen."

"Oh, he remembers that very well," said Kate. "But all the same... we think it might be a good idea if he has a separate dressing room for the rest of the tour. So there are no more... misunderstandings."

"Oh, there's no misunderstanding here," said Pete. "I understand all too well what he's doing, and why. And you can tell him that."

He mellowed slightly. "Sorry if I'm taking it out on you, though. None of this is your fault. And yes, separate dressing rooms sound like a very good idea."

He turned to his bandmates, "Okay, let's get out there and press the flesh."

# Lightning Never Strikes Twice

The next day the band were gathered in a cheap rehearsal room in Liverpool for another run-through of the show. Jane had grumbled to me privately that this wasn't normal. Normally, you stop rehearsing once the tour's actually started, and actual professionals only need a couple of days' rehearsal together before a tour anyway – the musicians are expected to have learned the parts on their own time, and to just quickly make sure everyone was on the same page together.

However, that was her experience of working with other professional musicians who toured regularly, and while the opening night had gone okay, it was clear that the actual members of the Cillas were still far from professional touring standard.

Robert, of course, had cried off from the rehearsal, claiming he was going to learn the music to "The Looking Glass", and that he knew all his parts for the rest of the show. And, to be fair to him, he did, more or less. He knew the tunes, at least, and he had a teleprompter to tell him what to say and what the words were, and so all he had to do was show up and be the focus of attention, which he was surprisingly good at for someone who seemed to have no attention span himself.

Without him in the room, the atmosphere lightened considerably compared to the way it had recently been. For all that the other three members of the Cillas were a bit sloppy and amateurish, they were also people who could at least have a bit of a laugh with each other and who fundamentally respected each other. I'd been truly touched by the way Sid and Pete had included Terry in their little gang so thoroughly that I didn't even know they'd never met each other before this tour. Being fucked over by Graham and Robert seemed to have made them bond straight away, and they were tight, as friends if not as a band.

Indeed, the atmosphere this time seemed more like a party than like a rehearsal. They'd got in a small audience of their friends – Chuck was there, again, but so was Mike Green, the old 80s DJ, who apparently still used the same hairdresser as he had back then – he had a dyed black mullet that made him look like a complete prick, and since he'd stood as an "Independent Moral Majority Anti-Immigration" candidate at the last election, I guessed that looks weren't deceptive, at least in this case. I was quite surprised that he'd even come and see a band with a black bloke like Sid in, let alone be friendly with them, but who can fathom the minds of racists?

Chuck was a little starstruck by Green, and went over to him to get his autograph in a paperback copy of a book Green had written about the Cillas. Chuck was gushing at Green, who was smiling and looking like he wanted to escape. I thought they made a lovely couple, the evangelical plagiarist and the racist has-been, and I hoped Chuck would talk to Green for simply hours.

But eventually, the band asked us to sit down, and the three Cilla instrumentalists, plus Andy, Simon, and Jane, ran through their entire set, tightening up tempos and reassigning instrumental parts. Terry was getting competent enough now that he could play the more complex bass lines and didn't need Jane to ghost them, which meant in turn that she could add in a few of the string parts that would otherwise have required her to have a third hand, and that in itself made a huge difference to the sound.

If you listen to those old Cillas records, you usually hear guitar, bass, and drums, often a second guitar or piano, but there's a sheen to them that comes from a trick their first producer, Pel Pelham, had used – you record a string section, put it through a reverb unit, then add only that reverb to the track, not the strings themselves. Jane had explained this to me, and it had sounded like a load of nonsense, but once I'd listened closely I could see that that was exactly what they'd done, and why those records which would otherwise have sounded like generic riffy rock sounded so... clean and shiny.

So Jane was able to add that sound, thanks to some artful sampling of the multitracks, and the difference was immediately apparent – they sounded fuller and richer.

They got through the set and seemed on a high, right up until the point that Andy looked at his phone.

"Oh shit. Oh shit oh shit oh shit," he said. "Oh fucking hell no."

"What's up, mate?" Pete asked.

"Just got a text from Janine. There's been an autopsy on Graham and the results are in. He was poisoned."

"What?!" Everyone in the room seemed to yell, almost simultaneously.

"Caffeine poisoning, apparently," Andy said, still reading from his screen. "He was allergic to it, and someone put some in his water bottle. Crushed up caffeine tablet. He only ingested the equivalent of half a cup of tea, but it was enough to kill him. Poor sod."

He looked up. "I'm going to have to call Janine. I guess that's rehearsal over for the day."

He left the room, phone held up to his ear, and the other band members stood there in shock. Most of them were still holding their instruments, and it took a good minute or two for them to even thing to start packing them away into their guitar cases.

Eventually, though, they pulled themselves together enough to start packing up, and the atmosphere returned to normal surprisingly quickly. Pete eventually said "I didn't even know he was allergic."

"You must have realised that he avoided caffeine all the time?" Terry asked.

"Well he was a Mormon, wasn't he? They're not allowed it."

"He was a Mormon? Then how come he used to get pissed all the time?" Sid said."He used to not drink anything that *wasn't* alcoholic. Said it was a waste of time when there was beer left undrunk in the world."

I jumped in there. "I know a load of Muslims who drink. My mate Mo often texts me saying 'I'm in the Mosque but I'll be leaving in five minutes. Order us a pint of Newkie Brown?'"

"Yeah, but Muslims aren't Mormons, though, are they?" Terry pointed out, reasonably enough. "I mean, you can't just say they're the same because they both start with an M. That's racist, that is."

Okay, so maybe things hadn't gone back to normal just yet. "I meant because both of them ban alcohol..."

"I know," Terry laughed, "I was fucking with you. It's just... I didn't know he was Mormon. I mean, don't they have to wear all special underwear and that?"

"When did you go looking at Graham's pants, Tel?" Sid chipped in.

"Listen, me and Graham were consenting adults, and what we did with his pants is no-one's business but ours," Terry replied.

*Ho ho, very funny*, I thought to myself. Still, these were men in their seventies, I couldn't expect them to have the same attitudes as a woke twenty-year-old on Tumblr, and if they thought that being gay was funny, there wasn't much I was going to be able to do about it. I wasn't here to fix their opinions, I was here as a reporter, to write fluff stories about them that could be used to sell tickets. I had to remember that.

"He converted in the nineties," Chuck called over from the other side of the room, "after he met Janine." The band ignored him.

"Should we really be joking about this?" Pete said. "I mean, this is Graham's death we're talking about, and now it turns out he's been murdered. I mean, I know none of us liked the bugger, but we could show a little respect couldn't we?"

"Aye, I suppose you're right."

"I just don't understand why anyone would want to kill Graham," said Sid. "Like you say, none of us liked him, but we were making money from him, so it wouldn't be us – if we found him that hard to deal with, we'd just quit, not kill him. Janine seems to genuinely love him... no-one else we know was even around at that gig were they?"

"Well, other than all the roadies and fans and so on," Pete pointed out. "They're actual real people too, Sid."

Sid looked slightly ashamed. "You're right, of course. There were loads of people there who might have wanted to kill him, thinking about it."

"He was a complete arse to the roadies," said Terry. "And half of those fans he'd groped at one point or another. I'm amazed he was never Weinsteined."

"The papers wouldn't have cared enough about that for anyone to kick up a fuss about him," said Pete. "Bloke who used to be famous forty years ago groped a few arses – it's hardly a headline that's going to sell a million copies, is it?"

They all looked glum – I suspected more at the thought of their own lack of fame relative even to Graham than at anything else.

"I tell you one thing," said Terry, "I'm not going to take another sip from any of those water bottles on stage any more. Cans only for me. Unopened cans."

The others nodded. "Getting pissed on stage... it's what the Graham we knew in the seventies would have wanted," said Pete. Nobody laughed. "We'll drink a toast to him between songs."

I was still trying to make sense of all this. But one thing was very clear to me. It was all happening all over again. I was once again going to have to investigate the murder of a rich white male arsehole.

This was starting to become a habit.

# Metal Guru

I've spent a lot of time in recording studios over the last few years, since Jane and I got together. They're all a lot less glamorous than you would imagine. They tend to be in units on industrial estates on the outskirts of big cities, and to have much the same ambience as a minicab office – all off-white painted walls, dingy brown carpet, cheap coffee and no windows.

Bigger Sound in Manchester, where the Cillas' album was going to be recorded, was no exception. It was chosen mostly because the band were doing more tour dates in the North of England than anywhere else, so it was relatively convenient for them all to get to between shows, but it had a horribly oppressive atmosphere. It was just uphill from Strangeways Prison, but it frankly felt like the prison had been put there so if anyone actually escaped they'd take a look at all the grey, depressing buildings, most of them former warehouses now converted into shops selling car parts or cheap carpets, and immediately climb back over the walls and go back to their cheery cells.

The studio itself was in the cellar of one of these horrible grey buildings, and being underground it was lit entirely by horrible fluorescent lights. I got the feeling that no expense had been paid when it came to choosing this venue as the home base for the Cillas for the next few weeks.

After going down the stairs, you're in a largeish underground building which has five main areas. There's a small room about the size of a public toilet cubicle with a single mic in it, which is used for recording vocals. And next to that there's a much larger room with a drum kit and amps, used for recording live musicians.

Both of these are in darkness, except when being used, and have glass windows through which they can be seen from the control room. This is mostly filled up by a couple of leather couches, a mixing desk, and a bunch of wooden shelves containing random bits of electronic gear. And acting as a corridor between the live room and the control room, there's a kitchen, with a tiny room at the other end containing a toilet.

On the first day in the studio, the musicians (other than Robert, who hadn't yet arrived) made their way into the live room and started setting up. This was actually quite unusual in my experience – normally the only person who actually plays in the live room is the drummer, with guitarists mostly sitting in the control room and plugging their guitars directly into the mixing board, while the keyboardist is usually playing into a computer. But apparently the Cillas felt like they should be playing together as a band, since all their studio experience had been in the old days of analogue tape, when the performance on the record bore some resemblance to what had actually happened.

The engineer, Scott, had gone into the live room as well, so I was sat on my own in the control room, drinking bad coffee and watching them through the window, when the producer turned up.

Jeff Washington looked like he could have had a job running an Internet radio show about conspiracy theories. He was one of those big, pork-faced, American white cis men who look like they've been carved out of pink jelly. He had a grey mullet and a pair of horn-rimmed glasses that I'm sure he thought made him look intellectual. He wasn't actually wearing a Hawaiian shirt, but I got the impression that that could change at any time.

He came up to me and shook my hand, crushing the bones in my knuckles, and smiled broadly. "Hi! You must be Sarah! I've heard so much about you! You're the reporter, right? I'll have to be careful not to spill any secrets around you!"

I got the distinct feeling that he was incapable of finishing a sentence without an exclamation mark. He had a loud, gravelly, voice, and he stunk of that particular kind of very expensive aftershave that manages to smell almost identical to very cheap aftershave.

"So what's your role in the organisation, Mr. Washington?"

"Oh, call me Jeff, please! Mr. Washington's my father! Well, the job title is producer, but I don't need to tell you that Robert Michaels doesn't really need a producer. Who could produce him? Really, I'm just here to communicate between Robert and the rest of the world. Robert is a... sensitive soul, and he's not used to dealing with people. Me, I'm a people person, as you can probably tell!"

"I see... so you're..."

"His collaborator. His partner. I co-wrote the songs with him, and I'm co-producing the album with him. I'm taking all the drudge work from him, freeing that profound mind of his to focus on higher things!"

This bloke was going to get on really well with Chuck.

He wasn't, unfortunately, going to get on as well with the band members. He walked into the live room and clapped his hands.

"Everybody? Everybody? Hi, I'm Jeff, and I'm going to be producing this session for you!"

"Where's Rob?" Terry asked.

"Robert is working on his parts separately. Don't worry, he's going to be fully involved in the new recordings. Today, we're going to work on one of his songs – 'The Spirit of You'. So if you could all put your headphones on and get round the mics, I'll teach you your vocal parts."

"Vocal parts?" Pete asked. "Shouldn't we be cutting the backing track before that?"

"Oh heavens, did no-one say?" Jeff looked horrified, as if this was the worst catastrophe in the world. "There's been some sort of colossal misunderstanding! The backing tracks are already recorded! Robert and I did them all last month, with some of the finest session players in the world!"

Pete looked like he was about to explode. "Really? Really? This is supposed to be a Cillas album, but it doesn't have the Cillas on it anywhere except as vocalists? How is this our album, Jeff?"

"This is hopefully the first album of a multi-record contract. We'll have more time on the next one, you can play your own parts then. But is this really any different from when you did *Goodbye Dragon*? That was just Robert and his collaborator for much of it, wasn't it?"

The other band members looked awkward, but said nothing and allowed Pete to speak for them.

"That was Robert and *me*. I'm a fucking *member of the band*. No offence, Jeff, but none of us have met you before. Yeah, Sid didn't do much on that album, but he was in a fucking state after his mate had died. It's not the same thing at all."

"Look, I know this is not what you'd have thought of as ideal, but remember a week ago there was no record deal, and the album's got to be out in a month. Can you just work with me here?"

"It's working *with* you that we want to do – work with you as opposed to just have you do everything."

"Look, I completely understand, and if you've got any songs you'd like to add to the album..."

Terry jumped in at this point, taking Pete's side. "What *I* want to add is any sort of creative input whatsoever," he said. "I don't know about *Goodbye Dragon* – I'd left the band by then – but this was *my* band. *I* was the one who formed it. I invited Robert and Ray into the band in the first place. And when we made records – when we made *hit* records, which I don't think you've ever done, have you? – we did it as a band, not as Robert Michaels and the Sidemen. That bass intro on 'Rumble Rabble'? I came up with that by meself. It wasn't something anyone wrote for me, and I played it, on an actual bass, not some outside producer pissing around on a synth."

"And that was great, for 1971," Jeff said, as unctuously as possible, "but for 2018 we need to be a little more structured than that. Studio time is money, and just in the time we've taken over this discussion we've wasted five hundred dollars of the record company's money. Look, at least listen to the track, will you?"

The band came through, and Jeff cued up a track on the computer, and it came through the massive speakers at the top corners of the glass window.

"What *is* this shit?" Pete asked after a minute or so.

"This is fucking abysmal," said Terry. "We're not the fucking Carpenters. We're a rock and roll band. This has no balls."

I have to say I took the band's side here. I don't know much about the realities of the music industry – Jane turns up, plays, and comes home, and she doesn't really talk about her work much – but I know what sounds good, and this sounded like some mid-90s Lighthouse Family shit or something. It was barely even music.

I was dreading the row that I could see brewing, but something worse happened then. Janine and Kate entered. Together.

# School's Out

They'd brought with them the two men I least wanted to see, Chuck the fanboy and Mike Green the racist DJ. I couldn't understand why they'd all come, and I certainly couldn't understand why they'd come in together. Janine should have had no reason even to be there – after all, her husband was dead, so he could hardly be on the album – while Kate was Robert's wife and it didn't make sense for her to be there without him.

But even more than that, I couldn't understand why everyone in the studio seemed immediately to snap to attention as they came in. What exactly was going on here?

"How's it going?" Kate asked.

"Not good," said Jeff. "We've got a bunch of snowflakes here, apparently."

"What the fuck is that supposed to mean?" Pete asked, and Jeff snapped off the talkback which he'd left on – whether accidentally or not I wouldn't want to guess. He turned back to the two women, his attitude completely different from the way he'd talked to me or to the band. He was now completely serious, all business, as if Kate and Janine mattered in a way none of the rest of us did.

"I knew this would happen," Jeff said. "You've not talked to them properly, have you?"

"Us talk to them?" Janine said. "Surely it's your job as the producer to explain the situation to them."

"I did. But... they're still thinking of themselves as a band. Like they're the bloody Beatles or something. I don't even know why they're here, to be honest. Why don't you just let me and Robert make the record by ourselves?"

Janine sighed. "Look, I'm not letting the band name be used on a Robert Michaels solo album. My husband was the voice of the Cillas. And yes, he's gone, but I'm not letting Robert erase him from history and claim to be the only one who did anything. We have the full band on there, precisely so no-one can say the Cillas were just Robert Michaels."

"But no-one would say that anyway," said Jeff. "After all, I'm all over the recordings. It's not like they're actual solo tracks."

"No, but that's how they'd be perceived. The Cillas were Graham, and Robert, and some other blokes. Now Graham's dead, they have to remain Robert and some other blokes; they can't just be Robert."

"That's what all this is about, really, isn't it?" Kate said with a snarl. "You don't care about 'preserving the value of the trademark' or any of that nonsense. What you want is for Robert to be minimised."

"It's all about preserving the value of the trademark!" Janine exclaimed. "If the Cillas name becomes interchangeable with Robert's name, then it loses its value, and you stop licensing the name. Which is what you want, isn't it? To have a hundred percent rather than fifty percent."

"Fifty percent?  He doesn't get a percentage, he gets a salary. Which is ridiculous as well."

"He gets a salary and owns fifty percent of the company."

"But right now he's doing a hundred percent of the work."

I thought about how lazy Robert was being, and how the other band members were working their bollocks off, but didn't say anything to interrupt them.

"Look," said Janine, "we made an agreement before the start of the tour that all the profits would go back into the organisation, and that Robert would get a salary on top of that. I don't see why that should change now."

"That was before all the publicity which Robert got by doing this album.  All that publicity from the album increases ticket sales, so of course Robert should now be on a percentage rather than just a salary."

"It's not 'just' a salary, and you know it.  You know as well as I do that he gets half the money from the company, and I get half the money."

I decided to get out of the room and go and sit in the toilet for a bit, to get away from the hostility. It was all getting a bit much.

I sat down and tried to get my head together, and It was only then that it really hit me. These two were talking about the band name being owned by Janine and Robert – which meant the other band members didn't own any of it. They weren't a band at all, legally – they were a bunch of hired hands, getting paid a salary by the company which owned the name, and which they had no control over.

I decided that I'd have to have a proper word with the band about all this. It was fair enough, I thought, that Jane just got a flat fee – after all, she wasn't even born when the records were made. The audiences weren't there to see her, they were there to see the four principals. But how could Terry, Sid, or Pete just be on a wage?

I mean, they were the band – they were the only people on the tour who'd been advertised as being there when people bought their tickets, even. Yes, Robert was now the lead singer, but that didn't mean the other three were hired hands who could be sacked as easily as the sound engineer.

I was actually finding this all quite upsetting. I knew that the re-union was for money rather than for the love of the art, but I couldn't help but think that there was something a bit dishonest about all this. People were paying money to see a band, and yet what was on stage wasn't really a band at all, but a boss and three of his assistants.

I wondered if Beth and Claire knew about this, but decided they'd probably known all along. For all their utterly sincere fandom of the band, they were also thoroughly cynical about the individual members and their motives. They seemed to know everything and to love the band for its faults. Must be a nice attitude to be able to have, I thought to myself.

As for the other fans... well, Chuck had made no secret of thinking Robert the only important one.

And I thought some more and realised that of course Graham and Robert were the only ones who'd been in the band throughout their original tenure – Terry, Sid, and Pete had never all played with each other – and that since Graham was dead now, maybe in Robert's eyes that *did* make him the Cillas. Was it like the Ship of Theseus – in which case we could see Jane, Andy, and Simon going out as the Cillas in twenty years, when Robert, Terry, Sid, and Pete were all dead? Or was it about continuity, in which case the band was just Robert?

And then I remembered that there'd been that single, fateful Cillas reunion gig without Robert but with Graham. Would that make Graham the only one who was in the band throughout, which would mean that the Cillas as a band were already dead?

Or was it just a trademark that could be applied to any group of people who got the license? That certainly appeared to be the logic that Janine was working off. Maybe it made no more sense to think about "the Cillas" as a group of people than it did to think about IBM or Microsoft as a group of people?

So what were all these fans following? Beth and Claire with their geeky enthusiasm about every aspect of the band members, or Chuck with his controlling, persnickety, pedantry? They were following something, but what that thing was could change totally without them caring, it seemed.

But then, that was true of football teams or soap operas as well, wasn't it? I supposed that was a thing about fandom, when you came down to it – it was supporting a brand name, not the art or the individual. A rather depressing thought, really, but probably true for all that. I tried to think of any fandom that wasn't, in the end, supporting a trademark rather than anything else, and I drew a blank.

But after some more thought, I realised that wasn't the point. The point of fandom wasn't to support the artists, it was to provide a shared reference point that could be used for creativity. It was a source for memes, for gifs, for fanfic – for shared jokes and a basis for friendships. The band weren't the point – they were just the grit in the oyster, the stone in the stone soup. I wondered if that was why bands all seemed to prefer Chuck's type of fandom: the anal tabulation of facts. It rejected any kind of creativity or joy, but at least it was about *the band* as individuals and not about ideas that could apply as well to different people playing those same songs.

Probably, I thought. If men were given the choice between women's joy or their own egos, they'd choose the egos every time, without even realising there was a question to be answered.

But these band members weren't allowed an ego, not any more, I realised as I came back into the studio and saw the band busily taking orders from Jeff. Now that their bosses had finished arguing and carving up their future, the band were going to be guided through a take of a song they hated. They had no choice in the matter.

Mike Green actually came over to chat to me for a second and offered me his hand. I shook it, bemused, and he said "I'm told you're writing articles about the band. Great bunch of lads, aren't they?"

I smiled politely. "Yes, I suppose they are."

He nodded. "Such a shame about Graham. I was thinking of asking him to work on a charity record I'm putting out for the Countryside Alliance."

"The foxhunting people? I didn't know they were still going." I didn't tell him I was vegan.

"Oh yes, very much so. We're seeing some very promising movement in the direction of legalising traditional country pastimes. But that wasn't why I wanted to talk to you – I just thought you might be interested in my book on the Cillas, as background information for your articles."

He handed me a thin-looking paperback, with a rather cheesy cover showing the band in front of a yellow background. I flicked through – large type, lots of pictures, looked like the sort of information that you can get from ten minutes on Google these days. I smiled and thanked him.

"I've signed it, of course," he said.

I opened to the flyleaf, and saw it was signed "to the lovely Sarah, from one author to another, Greeny Green."

"Oh, thank you!" I said, though I've never understood why people want someone to scribble in their books.

"My pleasure," he said. "That'll be ten pounds for the book."

I started to laugh, and then realised he wasn't joking. I wondered whether to make a fuss or not, and decided it would be worth the tenner just to shut wankface up, so I rooted in my bag for my purse, and managed to get together ten quid in shrapnel, which I handed over to him. I stuck the book in my bag, and he walked off.

I looked over at Chuck, who was openly smirking at me. I stared daggers at him, but he obviously found this the funniest thing in the world, so I turned away and started to pay attention instead to what was going on in the vocal booth. The band were making a fuss, as Robert still wasn't there.

"Look, what the fuck's Robert up to?" Terry asked. "We never see him except when we're on stage, and now he's not even turning up to the recording sessions?"

Kate tried to be conciliatory. "Robert's... well, he's shy about doing his vocals in front of you all..."

Sid laughed. "Robert? Shy? That's a first!"

"No, honestly, he is. He's not sung or played in decades, and while he can cover up the flaws in a live situation... he doesn't want you all to see him having difficulty, or having to fix dud notes with autotune."

"Ooh, ooh, I'm the same!" Pete said. "I can't possibly have any of you in here while I'm singing my backing vocal parts, in case I cough and you all laugh at me. Out! Out! While I work my musical magic. I can't have you peasants affecting my beautiful art." He placed the back of his hand against his forehead, melodramatically. "I can't be doing with his diva bullshit. Some of us are fucking professionals."

"Yes, yes, very funny," said Jeff Washington. "The fact remains, Robert wants to do his sessions alone, and he's asked me to supervise the sessions with the rest of you."

"Hear that, lads?" said Pete. "We need supervision. Stop throwing paper planes, teacher's here!"

The others laughed. Jeff was having difficulty controlling his temper, and both Terry and Sid were loving his discomfort.

Pete said, more seriously. "Look, I joined the Cillas, not the fucking Jeff Washington band. This is meant to be our record, not yours. What about doing some of *our* sodding songs?"

"Look, no offence mate, but the only member of the Cillas who ever wrote a hit record was Robert Michaels —"

"And Ray Evans."

"What?"

"Ray Evans. He wrote the hits."

"Yeah, but Ray Evans has been dead forty years. Robert's the only one of you who's actually capable of writing songs. And he's decided to write these songs with me, and those are the songs we're doing."

"So he wrote those songs 'with you' did he?"

"Yes, with me."

"And what exactly was the split in the writing? Did you do the words and him the music, or did he do the words? Who did what? Because these don't sound like Cillas songs at all."

"We both did both. Sometimes I'd come up with a chord progression, then he'd write the melody, then I'd do lyrics. Sometimes he'd come in with a lyrical idea and we'd workshop it together. It depended on the song."

"And you wrote these twelve songs together in less than a week, did you? Together?"

"No, it wasn't all done then. As soon as the reunion started being discussed Robert got in touch with me to see about doing a new album. We spent a few weeks knocking ideas around before the rehearsals for the tour even started."

"So why weren't we told about any of this then?"

At this point Kate interrupted. "Look... I'm going to be honest with you because I'm sick of managing your feelings. Frankly, the original plan was to just have Robert and Graham on it. The rest of you are expendable sidemen, those two were the Cillas. Now since Graham fucked us over by dying, we need the rest of you to use the Cillas' name, but that's all we need; the name."

I'd been worried about this kind of attitude, but I hadn't expected to see it so blatantly. Most of the people in the organisation who had been expressing opinions like that had been a little more circumspect about it, and I was quite shocked to see the callousness in the way Kate was expressing herself.

Surprisingly, Janine seemed okay with this discussion of how inconvenient her husband had been by dying, and I wondered if the rumours Chuck had mentioned about her being a gold-digger might not have a tiny bit of truth in them.

Pete continued. "Why? Why do you need the rest of us? You could still do it perfectly well with just Robert and not bother with us at all. Why go through this whole charade?"

"We might not need you legally, but it gives it legitimacy. It's not like the Beatles or something, it doesn't actually have to be John, Paul, George, and Ringo, but we need to have some lot of old blokes who used to be in the band to stick on the photo in the booklet to keep the fans happy. Otherwise the message boards will just start having flame wars, and all the YouTube videos will get trolling comments under them. That sort of thing eventually becomes bad PR. Look, I'd rather you sang your parts and got your credit legitimately, but really all you have to do is smile and keep your mouth shut. You got it now?"

"Yes. Yes, I've got it," said Pete, and took his headphones off and walked out of the vocal booth. The others looked bemused, and then followed him as he stormed out of the studio.

"Don't worry," said Kate to Jeff, "they'll be back tomorrow," and I had the sad feeling she was probably right.

# The Golden Age of Rock 'n' Roll

I could sort of understand, in a way, why Pete and Sid weren't "full members" of the band. They'd joined after the band's early hits, and they'd not worked through the hard slog of playing pub and club gigs, getting rejected by record companies, sleeping in the back of a Transit van, and all the other stuff that band members had to do when they were first starting up. They'd joined a group of pop stars, and could presumably rely on a steady income from the job while they were in it. It was fair, sort of, that they wouldn't get the same share of the profits, at least if you accept the basics of capitalism.

Terry and Dave were a different matter, though. When they'd started, the Zillas had been Terry's band, not Robert or Graham's. He'd brought them together, and it had been his vision. And Dave had been the only really solid instrumentalist among them, at least at first.

Now, apparently Dave didn't want to have anything to do with the band he'd helped form any more, and that was fair enough. But Terry was a different matter. He was back in the band, and he should be getting an equal share of it, at least by my admittedly odd standards of fairness.

And until that row between Janine and Kate, it had honestly never occurred to me that they were doing anything other than splitting the money equally between the band members, maybe with Robert getting a bit of a veto because he was the songwriter. But now I'd discovered that Terry was completely cut out of the profits, and I wanted to talk to him about it.

I asked him to come and have a coffee with me, and he made a counter-offer of a beer, so we sat in a dingy pub that stank of old men's piss, and drank beer that tasted much the same as the pub smelled.

After some aimless chit-chat, I finally got round to talking about how he'd ended up leaving the band in the seventies.

He shifted nervously, but eventually replied "It was really Clive, our manager. He thought I was unprofessional. Just because I wasn't the greatest bass player in the world. I was perfectly competent by then, but he didn't care. He was the one who really gave the group its direction back then – he was the one who brought in Graham to be the frontman. I was the original lead singer, you know."

"Really?"

"Oh yeah. I was quite good. But even then I was getting pudgy and balding, and he didn't think a little bald bloke could ever be a pop star. Must have been kicking himself a few years later when Phil Collins came along – and I was far better than him. But yeah, he brought in Graham and wanted to kick me out altogether, but Ray and Dave wouldn't let him, so I ended up getting relegated to bass. And eventually he kicked me out like he'd always wanted."

"But why did he want to kick you out, once you were on bass?"

"Ah, Clive never liked me. I was never pretty enough for him. And once his mate Graham was in the band... well, it very quickly became three camps, rather than a gang like it had been originally. Graham and Clive on one side, Robert and Ray on the other, and me and Dave stuck in the middle. Clive and Graham wanted us to be the Sweet, while Robert and Ray wanted us to be the Beatles, you know? And all me and Dave wanted to do was to earn a living by playing music, maybe have a laugh. So Clive wanted to replace us with people who were younger and sexier... thin lads with good hair, rather than someone like me."

He laughed. "I never looked good in all the glitter and makeup and shit. I looked like a brickie in drag. It was Robert and Graham who were the lookers of the band. I'm sure Clive would have got rid of Ray, too, eventually, if he hadn't topped himself first. He just wanted the pretty boys."

I took a sip of my beer while I thought about how to respond to this. "So you think Ray killed himself, then?"

He nodded, sadly. "Aye. Aye, I suppose I do. The pop star life was never for him, really. He was such a sensitive lad. Absolutely lovely bloke, but he never had a girlfriend, never even had any friends except me and Robert. It must have been hell for him having to choose between us when Clive had me kicked out, but I can't blame the lad – I'd have done the same in his platform boots. When you have to choose between two mates, it makes a difference when choosing one of them means you'll be on *Top of the Pops* next week and the other one just means you'll be down the dole queue. I just wish I'd been able to be there for him."

He took a big swig of his beer, and I could see tears in his eyes. I waited for him to speak.

"So. Anyway. You wanted to talk about how I left?"

"Well, I wanted to know about... well, I suppose I'd call it your severance package. What did you get when you left the band?"

"Oh, I did quite well out of it. Thirty grand, cash in hand, in return for giving up all me royalties and any right to sue. It's not like I was going to sue them anyway, the daft buggers."

"Thirty grand?! That's it?!"

He smiled. "You have to remember, lass, thirty grand in 1971 was a bit more money than it is today. I bought meself a nice house and a decent car, and had quite a pile left over to spare. Plus of course I'd been saving me royalties anyway. And it was worth it to just leave all the stress behind. By the time I was out, Robert and Graham were already not speaking to each other. Fuck knows how they managed to stay together for another three years or whatever it was. Money talks, I suppose."

"But... don't you feel cheated? The others became millionaires!"

"Nah, they earned it. Frankly, I was a bit of a crappy bass player. It was Robert and Ray who did everything. They deserved the money."

"But... I mean, you played on 'Misty Lady'. That was a massive hit. Surely it rankles that you don't get any money at all from that?"

"Well, a little bit, but I just look at it like every other job. If I was a carpenter... remember that one? 'If I was a carpenter, and you were a lady'... No, you're too young... anyway, if I was a carpenter, I'd not get paid every time someone sat on a chair I made, would I?"

"That's true, but then you couldn't sell the same chair a million times over or whatever, could you?"

He chewed on his lip for a second. "No. you can't. But that doesn't make me hard done to. It makes Robert a lucky bastard, but that's not the same thing. I'd say Graham as well, but... well, what happened to him wasn't exactly lucky, was it?"

I thought about that for a second. No, it wasn't lucky for Graham – and it was suspicious how anyone that Robert couldn't ease out of the band ended up dead. Terry, Dave, and Pete had all been sacked at one time or another, but he'd not been able to sack Ray and Graham, and now he didn't have to.

I put that thought aside for the moment, and tried to concentrate on the issue at hand.

"But didn't you form the Cillas? Don't you feel bad that you don't own the name?"

"Well, we came up with the name together. I was going to call us the Zillas. Like Godzilla, you know? But Ray misheard it, and so the name was his as much as mine. You can't say I deserve it..."

I was finding it difficult to understand his attitude towards his intellectual property rights. I'm a writer, and so I pay attention to these things – it's how I make my money. And I was a tech journalist before the recent fall-out, so I ended up knowing a lot specifically about licensing of software and so on. If you're in a creative business, there are times when you want to make your work available for free, or to let people share it, but the cardinal rule is always, always, money flows towards the writer, and if someone's getting paid for something you do, you make sure it's you.

But then, I supposed that in the Cillas' day people hadn't really needed to worry about money in the same way. I mean, there'd been poverty of course, but there was full employment and houses were cheap. You didn't have to pay two-thirds of your income in rent to some dodgy landlord who owned half the town.

But I didn't want to get sidetracked onto Boomer entitlement, so I got back to the point.

"So, you just gave up on the whole 'being a rock star' thing, then?"

He laughed. "I was never a rock star. I mean, yes, going on *Top of the Pops* a couple of times was fun, but I never had the girls screaming after me – when you've got Graham and Robert in the same band there's not really any reason for them to scream at bloody Terry Pattison, is there? No-one even knew who me and Dave were – I don't remember if it even got mentioned in the *NME* when we were kicked out of the band."

"Did you not try to carry on in music?"

"Oh, I tried. Formed my own band – the Terry Pattison Corporation. Released one single, which sold something like five copies. Did a couple of gigs as support for Stackridge and Blodwyn Pig." He laughed, "You know, it's probably the dictionary definition of failure, when the flute player from Blodwyn Pig tells you 'Look mate, you're never going to get anywhere in this business, you're crap. Give up'."

I gaped, "That's awful!"

"No, it was just the truth. The truth sometimes hurts. We were a shit group. The Cillas were a good group, but I never kidded meself it was anything to do with me. I got lucky once, and you don't get that sort of luck twice. I made me pile, had a few nice memories and stories to tell the grandkids..." he chuckled, "well, I can tell them *some* of the stories, anyway..."

He swigged down the rest of his pint. "Well, anyway, love, I've got to get going, Lovely chatting with you. Nice of you to be interested in the memories of an old fart like me."

He walked out, and I remained in the pub, lost in thought, until "Misty Lady" came on the jukebox. When Terry's bass part started, I got up and left.

# Done Me Wrong All Right

While Terry seemed quite composed about the way Robert, Ray, and Graham had ripped him off, the same couldn't be said for Pete. I did meet Pete for actual coffee, and in every way his attitudes seemed to be the opposite of Terry's.

If I'd been asked before talking to the two of them, I'd have guessed that Terry would be the more resentful of the two. After all, the Cillas had been his band, which he had formed, and which had been taken away from him by people he'd invited to join the band. Pete, on the other hand, had only been a hired hand all along. He'd been a teenage musician who'd been invited to join the band after they were already famous; he'd only ever been on a salary, and never a full member. If you were going to guess who would have been more philosophical about it, he'd have been your guess.

If you'd guessed that way, though, you'd have been very wrong. I'd barely brought up the subject of how he felt about the royalty situation when he said "I can't talk about that."

"Why not?"

"I signed a non-disclosure agreement when I left the band."

"Really? Terry never mentioned anything about an NDA."

He laughed. "Yeah... no, Terry wouldn't have needed one. It was only me."

"How come?" I realised what I was saying. "I mean, obviously, you can't tell me anything that it covers, but could you maybe explain to me why you're covered and Terry isn't?"

He shook his head, and took a swig of his coffee. "No. No, I can't. I can't tell you why I left the band, and I can't tell you how much they paid me to sign the NDA, except that it wasn't enough."

"Is there anything you can say?"

"I can say that I was treated like shit, and I wasn't the only one. What Robert did to us, the way he screwed us out of what we were owed...I don't know if Ray forgave him, in the end, but I certainly haven't. And that's all I've got to say."

I couldn't get him to talk at all further about this. Clearly whatever had gone on between the two of them business-wise in 1976 was still a sore subject. But I was interested in what he meant about Ray. Everything I'd read about the band, and everything the other band members had said, suggested to me that Ray Evans had been one of the few people to make any real money from the band.

"What do you mean about Ray? I read that he was worth a couple of million when he died, and those are 1970s millions. I would have thought he did okay from the band?"

"Oh, Ray got... well, I won't say he got the money he was owed, but he got far more of his fair share of it than any of the rest of us did. It was the way Robert treated him that was the real tragedy there. He hurt that poor man so badly, and I don't know if he even realises himself what it was he did. I hope he doesn't, really. I'd hate to think anyone could deliberately do that to someone else."

"What do you mean?"

"Look... none of it's my business to talk about. I didn't know Ray well, and I don't want to intrude on his privacy, even after all this time. But... listen to the lyrics on those later albums, the ones from right before Ray died. I'm sure you'll be able to figure it out for yourself."

"Are there any in particular I should listen to? Did he write the words or did Robert? I've never been able to figure out who did what there. "

"Just listen to them. I can't say any more."

I took a bite of my Danish pastry, and tried to think of another angle of approach. He clearly wanted to talk about something, but he equally clearly didn't feel able to. I chewed thoughtfully, swallowed it down with a mouthful of coffee, and collected my thoughts.

"So, you don't want to talk about any of that business stuff... can you tell me what it was like recording *Goodbye Dragon*?"

"I don't remember."

"You don't remember?"

"You deaf as well as dumb?"

I'd obviously said something to rattle him – this was not him being touchy, this was him trying to upset me enough that I'd stop asking him questions he didn't want to answer.

"Cut the ableist shit out. Surely you must remember recording that album. For most of it it was just you and Robert in the studio, wasn't it? You must remember that."

"Do you remember some random two or three month period you spent at work forty years ago?"

"I wasn't even born forty years ago."

"Exactly. Forty years is a long time, and it's just my job. I went in, played my parts, went back to my flat. What more is there to say?"

"But surely... did you ever get involved in Robert's songwriting process?"

"Honestly, we all kept to ourselves by that point, and anyway I never saw Robert write a song in my life. He's a very private person. Doesn't let other people in."

I thought for a second. "But isn't he a very collaborative writer? I mean, he wrote all those songs with Ray, and now he's been writing with Jeff... I mean, surely he lets other people in to the songwriting process?"

"You'd have to ask him about it." He sighed. "Look, I really wish I could help you, but the NDA I signed when I left the band was... well, it was vicious. I'm not allowed to talk about Robert's mental health, or his sex life, or his songwriting process, or his production and arrangement techniques, or any aspect of the business side of things at all."

"And all of that... applies only to Robert?"

"There's some more general stuff about not bringing the band name into disrepute and that sort of thing, but most of it's just about Robert, yeah."

"Does Robert... have something to hide?"

He looked incredibly stressed. "You know I can't tell you that, even if I knew. But... he's supposed to be a musical genius, isn't he? A hermit who hasn't made a public appearance in forty years. Mentally fragile. Can you think of anyone like that who wouldn't want their secrets kept from the public?"

He took a swig of his coffee and winced. "That's the worst fucking coffee I've ever tasted, and I've drunk a lot of coffee in my time."

I was glad the subject had moved onto something less fraught, and eagerly jumped on the comment.

"I've noticed that. You seem to get through like a gallon of the stuff a day. I'm amazed you're not constantly wired."

He smiled. "It calms me down."

"What, really?"

"Yeah, I think I probably have ADHD, Never been diagnosed, mind, but I have all the symptoms. And one of the things about ADHD is that you react differently to stimulants. You know Ritalin, what they give to hyperactive kids?"

"Yeah."

"Basically the same stuff as speed."

"You're kidding!"

"No, swear down. And so loads of ADHD people end up using coke or speed to self-medicate. Or, in my case, caffeine." He took another swig of his apparently-awful beverage. "And most of the time that's a far better choice for me than those things. I still have a septum, and I'm not having to visit dealers to get some horrible shit that smells of cat piss. Although this tastes almost that bad anyway."

I made a mental note of this. I've often wondered if I'm ADD myself, or maybe on the spectrum, and I had noticed that I was able to think better when I'd drunk coffee.

In fact, I felt like the coffee I was drinking right then was helping me think – and in particular that it was helping me figure out the questions I needed to ask in order to get my thoughts straight. This stuff about a secret in the band's past was intriguing – and could it possibly explain why Graham had been murdered?

Except... certainly Pete was talking about this as if it was something between him and Robert, not Graham – he'd barely mentioned Graham at all. Unless Robert had similar problems with the other band members... or indeed unless Pete was trying to make me think the big problem had been with Robert. For that matter I only had his word that there even was an NDA at all.

"So, how did you get on with the other members. You say you didn't like Robert and didn't really know Ray. What about the others?"

He thought. "Well, Sid's sound of course. We joined at the same time, and he's a fucking great bass player. Moving him to lead guitar after Ray died really wasted him – he's fine on the guitar, of course, but we could just lock in with each other when he was on bass. The others used to be pricks about it, say it's because he's black and he's got rhythm, that kind of shit. I always stood up for him, though – we were the new boys together, you know?"

I nodded. "Yeah, I can tell you two still get on really well. How about Graham? How did you get on with him?"

He shifted in his seat. "Well... to tell you the truth, and I don't want to speak ill of the dead, but I always thought he was a bit of a prick."

He looked at his watch, stopped talking and got up. "I've got to go. Catch you later, yeah?"

He rushed out of the room without even waiting for me to say good-bye.

# Personality Crisis

For once, Robert had decided to grace the tour bus with his presence. Normally he'd travel on his own, while the other three travelled on the same bus as the backing musicians, crew, and assorted hangers-on like me (although the on-again off-again nature of the tour meant that often some or all of us would just make our own way to the gigs, depending on how far they were from our homes and how many days there were between shows).

And for once the band members seemed to be genuinely getting on with him, at least a little. There was a wary acceptance there, but even Pete had exchanged a few polite words with him.

The bus had a TV, and there was a filler clip show on, with Stuart Maconie and sundry comedians called Russell in their late thirties, all talking about how much they pretended to love things from before most of them were born, for money.

This particular offender was a "twenty greatest glam rock songs ever" one, and so of course the band were watching it raptly, in the hope that they'd do well. Robert had talked about the band's big Christmas single, "Santa's Got a Spacesuit", as his pension – apparently it brought him in nearly a quarter of a million pounds a year. And while none of the other band members saw anything like that much money – Terry was the only other current member who'd played on it, and most of the royalties from old songs come from songwriting rather than performance anyway – they all still felt some affection for it as the work of their team.

Personally, I never liked the song. I'm a bit of a Grinch anyway, and Christmas songs just bring up memories of dire family parties when I was a kid, running around in the back room of a pub with a bunch of cousins I didn't like while the adults ate egg mayonnaise sandwiches off paper plates.

In fact, being on the bus felt a bit like that, with everyone eating junk food. I popped a Pringle in my mouth and instantly regretted it. Those salty little bastards look so tempting, but the MSG in them is insta-migraine for me. I took a quick swig of Coke in the hope that the sugar and caffeine would offset the headache. Defeating junk food with the use of other junk food, that's me.

The TV had gone through Alvin Stardust, T-Rex and Mud, and it was now into the top ten glam singles of all time. Would the Cillas actually beat out Slade, Wizzard, or Bowie? Or would they be forgotten altogether, thrown into the memory hole like Gary Glitter?

As the strains of Suzi Quattro faded, we got our answer. There on the TV were Graham, Robert, Ray, Terry, and Dave – the Cillas, 1972 edition – dolled up in makeup, but with Santa hats and fake beards, on the *Top of the Pops* set, miming their way through their Christmas hit.

"They don't write them like this any more, eh Pete?" Terry joked.

"No, these days they have some actual tunes, Tel."

"Christ, Graham could sing though," said Sid, more to himself than to anyone else. "He really was good, wasn't he?"

"When he wasn't pissed out of his mind, yeah. I remember it took us all day to get him sober enough to record the vocal that day. Should have been a clue about the allergy then, really, that he wouldn't drink the coffee."

We all became quieter.

"I wonder where Dave is now," said Robert. "Haven't heard anything from him in years. I'd be interested to know what he thinks about us getting back together like this."

"I'm pretty sure Graham asked him to be involved in the reunion," said Sid. "Something about getting the original line-up back together. He only called me and Pete once Dave said no."

"It couldn't have been the original lineup anyway," said Terry, "not without Ray."

Pete sighed. "No, but Ray was apparently just as important to Graham as me or Sid. Or you, for that matter, Tel, given how he'd treated you. Did he tell you where Dave is now?"

"No, he said something about him not wanting to hear from anyone. Last I'd heard he'd become a Hare Krishna or something," said Terry. "Weird to think of old Dave the Rave banging a tambourine and singing in Indian."

"Maybe by now he's finally keeping time properly with that tambourine," muttered Robert.

"Don't." A single word from Pete.

"What?!"

"You know fucking well what. Dave was a decent drummer. I should know, I have to play his parts."

"You don't have to. No-one's forcing you. You know where the door is."

"I do. I also know where the bodies are buried, so don't talk to me like that."

"What?"

"I know about your little plan to carve up everything between you, Graham, and Jeff. I'm sorry your partner had to go and die so you were forced into working with us nobodies again. But since he is dead, you need us, so you can show us some fucking respect."

"I'm not disrespecting you."

"No, but you're disrespecting Dave. Who was a fuck of a good drummer, and who played his absolute arse off for this band."

"What difference does that make to you? You've never even met the man."

Pete smiled. "As far as you know."

"What's that supposed to mean?"

"What I said. That I've never met him *as far as you know.*"

"So have you, then? Met him?"

"None of your business."

"So why are you being like this? If you don't know him?"

"Because it shows what you think of the rest of us. You think of us as just unimportant sidemen, flunkies you can order about. And we're not. We're members of this band, we make proper creative contributions, and you have never fucking acknowledged that. You think you're the big man, Charlie big potato, and that we have to bow and scrape to you because your name's on the songwriting credits on the records and some hack in *Mojo* called you a genius in 1993, the month after he said that about Skip Spence and the month before he said it about Roky Erickson. You're not a genius. You're Robert fucking Michaels from Burnage, and I'm not going to get down on my knees and give you a blowjob because you think you deserve it. Start treating us with a little bit of fucking respect."

I wanted to applaud, even though I'd never seen most of the disrespectful behaviour myself.

Robert turned away. "I knew it was a bad idea to travel with the rest of you. I'll get my own transport to the next gig."

"You do that. Feel free to not turn up at all."

Terry looked distraught. "Why does this always have to happen? Two minutes ago we were laughing away at that video of us, and now all this. Why can't you two just fucking get on?"

"I don't want to get on with him," said Pete. "I don't want anything to do with him. I'm here to do my job, and I have to do it in the same room as him, but I don't need to be his mate. He can leave me alone, and I'll leave him alone, and I'm very happy with that arrangement."

"We're supposed to be a *band*," Terry said, plaintively. "You know. a *group*. We're supposed to be *mates*."

"Yeah, well, we're not, though, are we?" Pete replied. "Look, I get on fine with you, but I've only known you a couple of months. Sid's an old mate, but I'd not seen him since his wedding twenty years ago. And Robert's an arse. We're not mates. We're colleagues. And me, you, and Sid are hired hands. That's not a band. That's not a group. That's three workmen and their boss. We're not even as important as Andy – he gets to boss us about. No offence Andy."

"None taken," said Andy amiably.

"All I want," Pete said, "is to play me skins, get paid, and not have to deal with Robert's bullshit. I'll be friendly enough with you or Sid, because you're both good blokes as far as I can tell, but I don't have to be mates with Robert, and I'm not going to be."

"Why do you hate him so much, though?" Terry asked. "What's he actually done to you?"

"I don't hate him, I despise him," said Pete. "They're different things. And I can't talk about what he's done to me. Maybe he'll tell you, if you ask him nicely. Or maybe he'll just clam up again and do his acid casualty act some more. Funny how he only turns that on when he'd have to deal with something uncomfortable, eh?"

Robert glowered, and the rest of the journey was spent in silence.

# Little Willy

Jane and I had got in touch with Claire and Beth, who were going to be coming to that night's show, and asked them if they fancied coming out for a drink with us. This was partly for "research" – I wanted to get background stuff about the band, and they seemed to be tiny bright-haired encyclopaedias about the history of the Cillas – but it was also because the environment around the band was, frankly, the dictionary definition of toxic masculinity, and we were both getting sick of it. A few hours hanging around with some actual other women seemed like the most appealing idea in the world.

The bar was crowded and full of the kind of loud, obnoxious chatter you get when office parties collide with stag dos and the general shouty drunkenness of people who don't get drunk together often enough to have worked out their behaviour as a group.

I figured that the only way to cope with the situation would be to join in with them, and so resolved to get as drunk as possible as quickly as possible. I ordered a round for the people at the table (two weird fruity cocktail things for Claire and Beth, a pint of bitter for Jane, and a gin for me), and an extra double gin for myself which I necked before taking the tray over to them. It wasn't even a good gin – it left a nasty oily, aftertaste – but I could already feel myself becoming a little bit louder, and a little less overwhelmed by the racket in the bar.

When I got back to the table, Jane was deep in conversation with Claire and Beth, who clearly had tons of gossip about the band and their associates which they were desperate to impart. I put the tray down and sat with them.

"Yeah, well there's all sorts of rumours about that randy old perv," said Claire. "Most of us are pretty sure he was into young boys. Most of the managers were back then – just look at that bloke who used to look after the Bay City Rollers."

"Who's this?" I asked, wanting to get up to speed quickly.

"Clive Salisbury, the band's original manager," replied Claire. "A man so creepy he made Gary Glitter look like... well, like someone utterly non-creepy."

"But I've heard it was even worse than that," Beth chipped in. "The stuff I've heard. . . I don't even want to say it out loud."

"The tortoise?"

Beth shuddered. "Yeah, the tortoise."

I wasn't entirely sure if they were joking with us.

"So what's happened to him now?" I asked.

"He moved to Switzerland, at least at first," Claire said. "No-one knows where he's living now. There's some sort of arrangement involving shell corporations, and he's changed his name at least twice that we know of. He could be literally anywhere."

"My guess is Thailand," said Beth. "A lot of that lot went over there. Out of the reach of the long arm of Yewtree."

"It's not just Yewtree he'd have had to worry about."

"No, but that would have been enough by itself."

I decided that I wasn't going to ask any more questions about Clive Salisbury. The euphemisms and avoiding the subject would just be too much for me to cope with. Whatever he'd done in the past, it was before I was born, and some things aren't worth the nightmares.

"So, you two planning on going to many more of the shows?" I asked, changing the subject in a not-at-all completely blatant manner, definitely not giving the impression in any way that I was digging for obvious information rather than smoothly segueing into another area of conversation (this may be a lie).

"Excellent subject-changing there," said Claire. "Seven out of ten for the swerve."

"Sorry, was it that obvious I was uncomfortable?"

"Little bit, yeah. But that's okay. We like TMI, but we know it's not everyone's thing."

"Yeah, we'll be going to all the shows," said Beth.

"Must be an expensive business," I said. "I had a look at those ticket prices – did you mortgage your parents for them or something?"

Claire laughed. "Nah, we get comped in to most of them," she said, "one of the few perks of being a proper fan."

"Oh, do the band give you passes then?"

"No," said Beth, "it's the road crew, mostly. The band don't care about their women fans – at least not since they got old enough that their dicks stopped working."

I shuddered. Some mental images you don't want.

"The band only care about the nerdy blokes," said Claire. "They're the ones who are all 'oh Mr Michaels what a genius you are and can I ask you about take thirty-four of that B-side from 1971 please sir?'"

"Yeah, we take the piss," said Beth. "Men don't tend to like that. It unnerves them."

"Plus, we know the embarrassing stuff," said Claire. "We're not going to ask them about what mics they used to record a drum part, we're going to ask them about whether Robert really did sleep with Ray that one time, or why Graham's second wife made him convert to Mormonism."

"Not that we're not interested in the music," said Beth. "It's just..."

"Don't worry, I understand completely," I said, thinking about my own ventures into bandoms in the past, and some fanfic I wrote when I was thirteen that I sincerely hope has disappeared from the Internet forever.

"But people like Chuck," Claire said, "or that arsehole Green – a word of advice about him, by the way: don't let him get his hands anywhere near you. The dirty fucking perv will put them everywhere. Though he might not, thinking about it – I'm pretty sure you're too old for him."

Well, there was a pleasant image.

Speaking of pleasant images, Beth's follow-on wasn't much nicer. "Those kind of men, they treat facts about a band as a dick-measuring contest. The more details they know about what kind of dust was on the microphones in 1972, the better. Green and Chuck do it all the time. Something to compensate for."

I didn't want to get into my rant about not mocking people for their body parts, so I tried to steer them back round to the stuff I didn't properly understand about the band.

"So, you seem to know everything about the band-members' pasts," I said "So do you happen to know why Pete got sacked? I tried asking about it, but he shut me down."

"Ah, yes," said Beth, "he would."

"It's simple," said Claire, "he got fired because he argued with Robert, and Robert can't cope with anyone telling him he's wrong."

"That makes sense," I said. "Bit disappointing, though. I was hoping there was some kind of juicy scandal around him."

"Oh no," said Beth, "that was Dave, the original drummer."

"Oh really?" I was all ears now.

"Yeah. You see, he'd been sleeping with Ray. But then he discovered that Ray was secretly in love with someone else, and broke up with him and quit. We've never been able to find out who it was who Ray was boning though."

"Well, they might not have been boning," said Claire.

"That's true," said Beth, "but it would make most of the fanfic a lot less fun if they weren't. But yeah, Ray was in love with someone else, Dave found out and quit, and then they fired Terry because he was only in the band because he was Dave's mate."

"But didn't Terry start the band in the first place?" I asked.

"Oh yeah, he got the band together, but most of them didn't like him very much. But he and Dave were super-close. They were like BFFs or something."

"Weird how they stopped talking to each other after they left the band though," said Claire.

"Not really," I said, "Not if Dave was gay – or bi, I suppose. Lots of homophobia and biphobia in the seventies. Terry might not have known until then."

"Now there's a depressing thought," said Jane. "I might be playing in a band with a raving phobe. Though he's never given the two of us any shit."

"Could just be that he's less arsey about women being together than men," I said. "You know, the whole fantasy thing. Or women being together just don't threaten toxic masculinity. Or it could just be that he's changed. People can change a lot in forty years."

"They don't seem to have changed all that much," said Jane. She was right, and that put a bit of a damper on things. We drank in silence.

# I Wish it Could be Christmas Every Day

The sleighbells were out, the Santa hats put on, and once again the Cillas were going through the motions of pretending to enjoy playing a song that two of them had pulled together in ten minutes, forty-five years ago, and which had been the bane of their existence ever since.

Even though it was only early October, everyone knew that the Christmas song would be the big draw for the tour. The Manchester Apollo gig was going to be the biggest til they hit London, if not in terms of raw audience numbers then in terms of enthusiasm.

We'd talked about how people will accept festive material from the start of autumn, but after New Year's they'd be unable to keep it in the setlist – and without their biggest hit they were also without the biggest reason for the audiences to come out, so they were milking the song as much as possible in the months leading up to Christmas.

(Personally, I felt grumpy about the way "Christmas" now meant "the month of December", when I'm enough of a traditionalist to think of most of that as "Advent" and the Christmas period as lasting from Christmas Day through to Twelfth Night. But I'm also enough of a realist to think that I'm probably the only person in the world who isn't actually a ninety-year old cis white man writing for the Torygraph who cares about that.)

"Okay, kiddies, are you ready for Santa?" Robert cried out. "Because it's chimney time!"

I looked from the side of the stage at Jane, stood there with a fake smile plastered on her face, Santa hat askew, shaking sleighbells with one hand while playing the string line with her other. She seemed almost to be enjoying herself, which was more than could be said for Sid and Pete, stuck playing a song that defined their band but which they'd had nothing to do with.

"Oh it's that time of year again, for turkey and mulled wine
A time when we all celebrate, because it's Christmas time.
And every boy and every girl keeps their eyes scrunched up tight
Cause they all know that Santa Claus is visiting tonight
And everyone sing along!"

They went into the chorus, but suddenly the sound became awful. There was some sort of atonal thrashing going on – an arrhythmic noise that was overpowering everything musical. The crowd were becoming restless, but I could see that whatever the noise was, the band members couldn't hear it – they were continuing to play as if nothing unusual was happening. Clearly the mixes in their monitors were fine, even if the audience mix wasn't.

Some of the front row of the audience were still singing along gamely, expecting the problem to be rectified, and the band had spotlights on their faces so they probably couldn't even tell that the audience were confused. But not as confused as I was, until Robert turned towards us and I saw that the racket perfectly matched what his hands were doing on the guitar.

It was him. He was just making random noise with his guitar. I went over the couple of steps to the sound engineer who was supervising the mix from the side of the stage. "Why's Robert making that racket? He's ruining everything!"

"Shit, is that what it is? I was trying to figure out what was going on." She pressed a button and the noise instantly stopped.

"Why was he doing that? Was he trying to sabotage the band?"

She looked shaken. "No, that was entirely my fault. Robert's instruments aren't meant to go into the front of house mix at all. He's just supposed to hold his guitar and thrash at it, not to actually be playing anything anyone can hear."

While Robert's racket had stopped, the audience were taking some time to get back into the music, and now – even though the problem itself had been fixed – the band were starting to notice the audience's confusion, and they were starting to get, not exactly sloppy, but a little bit hesitant.

I felt for them. After all, they literally had no idea what the problem was, and so they couldn't possibly have realised what was causing the unrest. I just hoped it didn't wreck the show altogether.

"Why do you even have his guitar plugged in at all, if it's that bad?" I asked the engineer.

"Oh, it's very simple," she said. "He needs to hear himself playing so he can sing. It's a psychological thing – a lot of people have it. You'd be surprised, really, how many famous musicians are the same, playing just for themselves and not for the front of house mix. So it has to go into the board so I can stick it in his in-ear monitor. None of the other band members ever get to hear it, and normally neither do the audience. I don't even record it when I'm recording the other tracks."

"You record the shows?"

"Oh yes, every night. Andy goes over them the next morning and looks for stuff that needs to be tightened up."

I nodded. That made sense actually. Poor Andy had to do all the work of keeping all the musicians together. I hoped the poor sod at least got decent pay for it.

"Did you record the show the night Graham died?"

She thought. "No, I wasn't in charge of the soundboard for that night. It was a BBC show, remember? They were recording it for the broadcast. I was there, to help them with the setup and the cues and that, but one of the BBC engineers was in charge of the recording."

"Do you think they'll still have a copy of it?"

"Oh, definitely. They never throw anything away any more. Digital storage is dirt cheap. Can't imagine it'd be worth listening to, though – they only did the one song before Graham died."

"No, I wasn't thinking of... never mind." She'd already turned away and was busy fiddling with knobs as the song finished and the next one came up. I felt bad for distracting her, even for a moment – dealing with a live sound mix is hard enough at the best of times, and with a band like the Cillas, where half of them were out of practice and being ghosted by other musicians covering the hard bits, it must have been like juggling flaming chainsaws.

And there was an extra part to deal with, I noticed. There was a grey-haired bloke on stage who I'd not seen before, looking like Jeremy Clarkson's dad in his denim shirt and jeans. He was standing at an extra mic that had been set up for him and cupping his hand to his ear. I asked Jane about him later, and she said he was some Legendary Old Rock Star who I should feel bad for not knowing, but my own view is that if I don't know about him, he can't be that legendary.

Anyway, the LORS was apparently visiting family in Manchester for Xmas – he lives in LA, as all LORSes do, but he has a brother there or something – and so he was slumming it and joining in with the band on "Misty Lady", singing Robert's old harmony line along with Andy while Robert sang Graham's part. I've seen bands do that kind of thing occasionally, and I've never understood why. It's not for the audience – the guest never adds anything to the song – and the audience is expected to just go mad because there's an extra person on stage pratting about.

This LORS could at least sing, though, even if he did have curly grey hair and a scrubby grey beard. And even if he did put his hands together in a prayer motion and half-bow at the audience, as if he was the fucking Dalai Lama or someone rather than someone who likely spent the years 1966 to 2017 inclusive snorting coke and having sex with underage girls.

(I'm not saying he did those things – I know nothing about him, not even his name, and I'm judging purely from looking at him for five minutes while he was on stage – but he definitely, definitely, did those things.)

And then at the end of the song, he stepped to the mic and spoke to the audience.

"I feel so very blessed, so honoured, to be here tonight in the presence of genius," he said. "That's a word we use too much, but tonight we're definitely in its presence. Ladies and gentlemen, applause please for the genius that is Robert Michaels, and his Cillas!"

He bowed again, and as he bowed, I could see Pete glaring at Robert, and wishing him dead.

# Angel Fingers (A Teen Ballad)

Andy walked to the front of the stage, and spoke into Robert's mic.

"Okay, tonight is, of course, a special night for all of us, but we're going to make it just a little bit more special."

The crowd murmured. What was going on?

"We've been doing the same songs every night so far, but tonight we're going to do something different. A song most of you will never have heard, but not a new one. Some of you may be aware that when the Cillas broke up, they were working on an album called *Rising Up*. That album was never finished, but a few of you may have heard some of the tapes through... naughty websites." He paused. "Don't worry, we won't tell on you."

The audience laughed. Claire was sitting up in her seat, on edge.

"Anyway, tonight we're going to play one of the songs from that album. We hope you like it. It's called 'Catch and Return'."

Claire actually screamed. It was only a muffled one, but that's definitely what she did. This apparently really was going to be something special.

It was... astonishing. It was nothing like any of the music they'd been playing so far. Most of the Cillas' stuff was stompy, guitar-driven, fuzzy glam rock. This bore no resemblance to it, structurally or in the instrumentation. There were no guitars at all – Andy and Sid were just stood at their mics, singing, while Robert had switched to a keyboard.

Simon had moved over to a vibraphone that was set up next to his kit, just behind Jane, and played a simple single-line melody, while

113

Jane and Terry played interlocking bass parts. I wish I had the musical understanding to explain on a technical level what it was that made this music so distinctive, but it was immediately apparent to me that this was nothing like anything else the band had done.

"You were chasing," sang Robert, "and we finally caught you, caught you but now you've gone again "

This was even more advanced than the songs I'd heard from *Good-bye Dragon*. This was barely rock or pop music at all. But it wasn't proggy wank either, even though it was from 1976. This was a proper tune.

The backing vocals came in, each member singing a different vocal line, but somehow all sounding clear and distinct.

I looked at them all there in the darkness, the spotlights picking out their faces. And at Jane, Andy, and Simon, still enveloped in the darkness but doing most of the work. I could feel the hairs on my arms starting to stand up, as I got a visceral sense of wonder that these flawed, human people – old men, for the most part, with body odour and bad breath and all the other problems that old men get – were capable of producing music so inhumanly beautiful. I almost got a feeling of what Christians mean about the connection between the physical and the divine. Maybe that was what made Chuck such a fan.

How could the same people switch between producing this absolute beauty and stuff like "She's My Lady "? That one's a lot of fun, if you can avoid thinking about the dodgy sexual politics, but it's earthy, human fun. But this was something else altogether.

I looked at Jane, her hands frantically moving over the keys, playing a bass part with one hand and a string part with the other, and wondered how she managed not to be moved by this. To perform this music, she had to treat it as a technical exercise. How you could think about it in terms of moving your fingers and still make it musical was something that still fascinated me. As a writer, I could never get a sentence done if I thought in terms of "now I am pressing the 'a' key and Shift, now I am pressing the space bar", but from what I could tell about Jane she literally had to do just that on this sort of material.

When they were playing the rockier, simpler, stuff, apparently, she could just use her muscle memory and let it flow, like I do when I'm typing. But this kind of stuff, with the complex counterpoints and time signature changes, was the opposite – she couldn't let herself feel the music, she had to just count beats and pay attention to the technical aspects of what she was doing. It was, she'd told me, why she hadn't gone the classical route – she'd have had to do that kind of thing all the time, and never let herself just get carried away by the music. It seemed sad to me, and she told me that wasn't how it was for most musicians, but it was how her brain worked.

But she was managing to play this intricate stuff. Robert was moving his hands on his keyboard, but I've been around Jane long enough that I can tell how her hands sound on the keys, and all of what I was hearing keyboard-wise was coming from her. You'd think that you wouldn't be able to tell that sort of thing – after all, electronic keyboards are basically just switches that you turn on and off, and so two people playing the same part should sound exactly the same – but Jane told me that it was perfectly normal to be able to pick out a player that you're familiar with.

But *why* was Robert not playing properly? It looked like he was playing, but he wasn't in the mix. But he'd written the song. The others needed people to carry them a bit because they were out of practice, but they were playing complicated parts, and usually parts they hadn't written themselves. Robert had written every note he was playing, but he was the only member of the band whose instrument wasn't in the mix at all.

And even his vocal... he was almost speak-singing the parts, not singing them properly. It worked, more or less, but only because the rest of the band sounded so bloody good. What, exactly, was going on with this man?

But I could see why they called him a genius, if he could write this kind of thing.

But while he'd written it, he didn't seem to be responding to it at all. He was sat there expressionless, moving his hands on his dummy keyboard, singing this gorgeous music without apparently even realising it was special. The only one on the stage who seemed to be responding to it at all was Pete.

When Pete plays drums, normally he's something like Animal from the Muppets – arms everywhere, shaking wildly, thrashing his hair in front of his face. He's a ball of energy, although he's not the steadiest drummer I've ever heard (Simon was in the band to ensure that they had a rock-steady backbeat while Pete did his thing). But here Pete was playing the only drum kit, rather than sharing the drum part with Simon, and he was playing with these tiny, precise movements. I've thought about it for a long time, and the only way I can describe it is that it looked like he was treating his playing as a prayer. He was playing with the same precision as Jane, but while Jane's precision was an intellectual one, Pete's was more intense – each time he hit a drum there was a sense of finality, like this is the right drum, the one that needed to be played at this precise moment.

It was really weird to watch, because this was a song written by a man Pete hated. Maybe he could separate the music and the song-writer. Maybe.

# The Secrets That You Keep

I'd decided it was probably worth my time to at least try to read Greeny Green's book on the Cillas. Not only was it useful background information for the job, but given my increasing suspicion that Graham's murder had something to do with something in the band's past, I wanted to get as much of an idea as possible of what had gone down between them.

The book was... it was embarrassingly badly written, to be honest, and I was astonished that it had got through the editorial process in what was a generally respected publishing house. But then, I suppose celebrity, even of the micro variety that Greeny has, had its privileges.

The book was written in a faux-jocular tone that read as if he'd been informed of the existence of the concept of "a joke", and hadn't really understood what one was, but thought he might as well give it a go. (And, in fact, you could say the same but for "book" instead of "joke "). It was stiff, mannered, and with no feel for basic things like sentence rhythm.

But on the other hand, the book at least had some sort of facts about the band in it, which is more than I could say about anything I'd seen other than Chuck's webpage – and I checked the acknowledgements and was completely unsurprised to see that Chuck was mentioned prominently as a fact-checker and source of information.

But the problem was... there was a narrative, and a set of facts, and the two didn't seem to be going together. And Green didn't seem to realise that they weren't going together. The narrative he was setting out had Robert Michaels as a transcendent genius who was carrying the rest of the band and repeatedly saving them from irrelevance, yet when you looked at the facts, without any preconceived "this man is a genius" notions, what you saw was an acid casualty who wasn't very good at playing his instrument and who kept sacking people whenever they got annoyed at his sloppy performances on stage.

All the quotes from anyone he interviewed talked about him being a gentle spirit, a soul who was too fragile for this world. But all the actions described looked like those of a monstrous control freak who couldn't cope with the mildest of disagreement. All the quotes, that is, except those from Graham, who Green seemed to want to position as the "other genius." Everyone else quoted in the book seemed to think of Graham as an irrelevance (though notably Graham was the only band member interviewed), but Green seemed as big a fan of him as Chuck was of Robert.

And this made me wonder about something: I knew that Green's book sales would have gone through the roof after Graham died. His book was the only one out there about the Cillas, and as far as I knew there were no books about Graham as a solo artist either. I have a friend who'd written a book about David Cassidy who said that when Cassidy had died my friend had made a thousand quid in a week from book sales. And Graham was definitely more famous than David Cassidy, who I'd literally never heard of before he died.

So had Green perhaps decided to give his royalties a little boost and kill Graham off? Could he have been that cynical – murdering a friend in order to boost his own career? I couldn't let go of the notion.

It seemed unlikely, but at the same time I honestly couldn't put it past him. The man was clearly a racist, and a misogynist, and a general all-round prick, and people like that tend to be narcissists more often than not. And I can say from unpleasant personal experience that narcissists don't really think of other people as being people.

I didn't want to think that badly of him, though. I still had some fond memories of him presenting *Top of the Pops* when I was a kid – and he was practically the only one of those presenters who wasn't now in prison for fiddling with little kids, so the fact that he was a bit of a racist arse didn't weigh quite so heavily in comparison. So I really wanted to find some reason why it couldn't have been him who'd killed Graham.

But the fact that his book had done so well off the back of Graham's death meant I couldn't put the idea out of my head. And a quick perusal of his Wikipedia page led me to think he probably needed the money. He'd filed for bankruptcy at least twice, and his fees for the appearances he'd made on the radio talking about Graham probably came in handy.

I remembered a piece I'd seen about him on the Daily Mash or one of those satire sites a couple of years back, after a few celebrities had died in the same week. "Police warn all pop stars to beware of Mike Green in case he kills again, after his twelfth appearance this month providing an instant obituary for a minor pop singer." The joke had been that all the celebrities had been being murdered by him, so he could go on the radio and collect the appearance fees. And now I was considering whether the joke had really been all that funny.

After all, he did have a reputation for providing obituaries for musicians at short notice, and they always seemed well prepared. And none of the musicians who were actually his friends – like that bloke who did the music for the 70s puppet show, or whatsisname who used to work with Andrew Lloyd Webber – none of them ever seemed to die suddenly, which given how many people probably wanted to kill them after their smug appearances on *Countdown* was a minor miracle in itself.

I was being stupid. This was getting to me too much now. How could TV's Pop Picker Greeny Green possibly be a serial killer?

Well, how could half of the staff of Radio One during his time there have been serial kid-rapists? He was from a time when celebrities could, quite literally, get away with murder. Maybe he had. Maybe he was continuing to do so, even now. He didn't seem like a murderer, but then neither had the last murderer I'd had to deal with.

I needed to think about this.

I did a bit more research – by which I mean following links from his Wikipedia page and Googling a bit – to see if he had any previous relationship with the band. It turned out he actually did – he'd made an album in the 80s of what he called "a rock tone poem", taking the poetry of A.E. Housman and the music of Elgar and trying to smash them together into a song cycle about the death of old England and the loss of the British Empire. Graham had been one of the guest vocalists on it, along with one of Buck's Fizz and a bloke with a beret from some band called Curiosity Killed the Cat who I'd never heard of. The 80s were weird, apparently.

I had a listen on YouTube to the track Graham had sung on. It was like anti-music, something so unlistenable that playing it would actually destroy some other piece of real music that was near it. And it was just stodgy, and pompous, and self-important. A man who could make a record like that was capable of anything – certainly of murder, if the way he had killed the song form so thoroughly was anything to go by.

But it showed that the two of them had connections going back thirty or more years. If Green did have a reason to kill Graham, maybe it dated back that far.

I picked up the book again and carried on reading, in the hope of finding a clue...

# Horror Movie

I couldn't understand it when I saw the text message flash up from Jane, who'd gone ahead to the soundcheck. The plan was that I was going to meet them at the gig itself, because the principals were going to be spending most of the day in business meetings to which I wasn't invited, and the three backing players were going to cover most of the soundcheck stuff between themselves, with the principals only popping in in the last few minutes for a quick run through of two songs they were adding to the set.

I assumed that if she was messaging me, it was just to say "I love you" or "remember to put the bins out" or something of that nature. Instead it just said "Jeffrey's dead. Everything's in complete chaos. Suspected murder."

It took me a second to think who Jeffrey was, before I remembered he was the producer who'd been working with Robert on the new album. As soon as I realised that, I felt my stomach collapse. I was only just getting over the killings on the island a few months earlier, and now this?

I tried phoning Jane, my hands shaking so much it took me three goes, but she wasn't answering. Fair enough in the circumstances, but it left me worried. What was going on? Graham's death had been bad enough, but now for Jeffrey to die as well? Was a serial killer stalking the Cillas?

And why Jeffrey of all people? He was the one person who could get the album out and get the band to have the proper comeback they wanted. He could make the difference between them breaking even and making millions. After all, Jeffrey was the only thing making the album even slightly possible. The relationship between Robert and the other band members had deteriorated to the point that they weren't speaking to each other, except on stage, and Robert wouldn't even record in the same room as the rest of them.

Jeffrey wasn't exactly loved by any of them, but there was no reason for anyone to want him dead. He'd seemed a bit of an arrogant arse, but no more so than anyone else in the rock music business seems to be. And he was actually getting stuff done for the band and making their comeback work. Maybe it was a jealous member of Slade or the Glitter Band who wanted him to be working with them instead?

I really needed to get out of the habit of making that sort of joke, especially if this kind of thing was going to keep happening. It's all very well talking about gallows humour, but that doesn't really excuse actual callousness. I'd only just been thinking to myself about how narcissists didn't really think other people counted as people, but was I any better, making jokes, even if only in my head, about the deaths of people I knew?

I was going to have to think a lot more about my attitudes to this kind of thing, but I was also going to have to seriously think about who could have done this, and mentally accusing the ex-members of third-rate washed-up glam bands wasn't going to help anyone at all. I knew from my experiences with the techbros that murder investigations can last long enough that more people would die, and this was the second murder to happen on this tour. If I wanted to prevent a third, I had an obligation to try to figure out what was going on.

And I suddenly thought... this was history repeating, wasn't it? The last time the band had worked on an album that was just Robert and a collaborator, one of the band had died just before it. That time it had been Ray, this time Graham. And then something had happened to split the band up, and if anything was going to split the band up again, it would be people getting murdered all around them.

Was someone trying to make the events of 1976 happen once more? That time had, after all, caused the band to record their best album – could a fan be trying to recreate the conditions that had led to that, so they could be sure of getting another *Goodbye Dragon*? Could that be what was going on?

It was obvious, after all, that the fans didn't care what happened to the band members so long as they got new music out of it. This whole thing could have been a *Boys From Brazil*-style attempt to bring someone back from the dead – in this case, the Robert Michaels of 1976.

I put that idea out of my head. It was possible, no doubt, but I was speculating on far too little evidence. I'd have to get to the venue, look after Jane, and maybe talk to the other band members. Gather facts, not wool.

Poor Jeffrey, though. I'd not liked him very much, but I didn't want to see him dead. Compared to half the people I'd met through Jane's work, he was almost a saint – just someone who was trying to do his job and get a record made, not someone who was groping his way through half the world's supply of teenage girls in a cocaine-fuelled frenzy. If everyone in the music business had been like him, there'd have been a lot more boring music in the world, but a hell of a lot fewer innocent casualties.

I got to the venue, and found it a lot less chaotic than the aftermath of Graham's death had been. Thinking about it, that made sense, of course – Robert was the only one here who'd spent more than a day or two in Jeffrey's company, while all of them had known Graham for decades, even if they'd been out of touch recently. I thought about how I'd feel if one of my old school friends I'd lost touch with died, and compared that mentally to how I'd feel about an editor who'd commissioned me a time or two, and the reactions here made sense.

Or at least, they did until I remembered my serial killer assumption. Maybe it comes from having already dealt with one of them, but my own thoughts when two people I'm working with get murdered immediately jump to "what if I'm the third?" That didn't seem to have occurred to anyone here, and I wasn't going to be the one to put the idea in their heads.

Jane wasn't crying this time, but she was clearly shaken. She was white-faced, and gripping her coffee cup too tightly, and when I went to hug her she waved me away – sometimes she doesn't want to be touched when she's overwhelmed. I held back, but hoped me being there would help her feel better.

I looked around, and most of the usual suspects were there – Chuck, Janine, Kate, and the band members had all turned up, and they were all looking ashen-faced. But one person was noticeable by his absence – Mike Green, the person I'd been suspecting. Had I figured out who the killer was?

# Yesterday's Hero

But while it was just possible that the mullety kipper DJ had killed Graham, I couldn't see him having killed this Jeffrey bloke anyway. His book was more likely to sell if the Cillas actually released a new album than if they didn't, after all. Unless... maybe he wanted to get involved in making the record? Maybe he was going to volunteer his "services" as a co-producer? I knew he made records, of a sort – I'd heard his song for the 2017 election, "Send Them Back, Nigel." Even the radio station he was a DJ on now had banned it, let alone the more popular ones he'd been on when he still had a career. But maybe he was delusional enough to think that the Cillas would recognise his talents and let him be involved in making the records.

But no, that didn't really make much sense, either. After all, Robert was a record producer himself. He didn't really need a co-producer – surely any competent engineer could guide him through using the modern production technology? Jane had often said that it was the engineers who did the real work in the studio anyway – the producer would say "we need a little more reverb on the snare" or something like that, but it was the engineers who chose the microphones, placed them, and added the effects chain that made it sound like an actual record rather than just some kids pissing around on instruments.

Robert could make the record without any assistance – and frankly his ego was such that it was hard to see him giving up any control to anyone else. I was actually amazed, thinking about it, that Jeff had been involved at all. Maybe Robert had killed Jeffrey because he wanted more reverb on the high notes or something?

I was just being ridiculous now. Jeff had been Robert's man, loyal to him rather than to the band as a whole. It couldn't have been

Robert. And the other band members had seemed to loathe Jeff, but it wasn't like killing him would suddenly give Pete and Sid the opportunity to come up with their own parts for the album – it just meant that the release would be delayed until the record company could get someone else they trusted to do Jeff's job of making the actual record. I didn't know the details of their contract with the label, but I couldn't imagine that that could be good for them financially.

Or could it? I decided that I'd better try to get hold of a copy of their contract at some point and see what it actually said. Would they even get paid anything extra if the album came out, or would it all go to Robert and to Graham's estate?

This was getting needlessly complicated. Maybe it wasn't anything to do with business or money or art at all. Maybe he had an ex who hated him, or someone else he worked with, or maybe it was just something random. Maybe someone just didn't like obnoxious mulletted spam-faced men. And then I realised – Graham had had a mullet too! Maybe I was facing... a mullet killer! In which case Green might be next! He might be a victim, not the killer! I had to warn him.

I was just about to get out my mobile and call him to warn him about the mullet-killer, and then I realised. I was going into a manic phase. I should have realised sooner, but I'd been under a lot of stress. I was obviously having a hyperbrain moment, when everything seems to be connected to everything else and I start seeing patterns that aren't there. I decided I'd need to call my GP and see about upping the dose on my meds, but for now the best thing I could do was to calm myself down as best I could and try not to think about any of this any more.

I did, though, congratulate myself on realising it was my illness talking. I had to laugh at the ridiculousness of it – imagining a mullet-killer – but I also had to not laugh too much. Going on a laughing jag wouldn't help my brain settle down right then.

I decided to try to meditate. I settled myself down in a quiet corner and started chanting my mantra under my breath, but soon Chuck came up and started bothering me.

"Trying to think about who the killer might be?" he asked. "Using that detective brain of yours to catch the crook?"

I glared at him. "No, I'm trying to stop myself having a major panic attack. Some of us see people getting murdered as a bad, thing, not just as an excuse for solving a puzzle."

He backed off, hands in the air in mock-surrender. "Okay, okay, be like that. I was just trying to be friendly."

"Well don't."

I felt like an arse almost straight away, but I didn't have the spoons for dealing with wankers like him. Not right then.

It didn't help that he'd been right. I'd not really been thinking about Jeffrey's death at all in any real sense. I wasn't seeing him as a person, with a life and interests and a family and friends, whose life had been taken from him. I hadn't thought about how that loss would affect all the other people in his life, how he maybe now had kids who didn't have a dad, or parents who'd lost their only child, or anything else. I'd just been thinking about his murder as a problem in logistics, trying to figure out who could have committed the act.

It was something I did all too often. I got entirely wrapped up in my own intellectual concerns and failed to understand the emotional impact those things could have on other people. And then I would snarl at other people for making the same mistake, but just doing it slightly more openly than I had.

I decided then and there that I was going to find out more about Jeffrey and his life, not to solve the murders – though I'd be entirely happy if I was able to do that, of course – but to make sure there was one more person out there who remembered Jeffrey the man, and who mourned him. He might be dead, but I'd make sure he left at least some small mark on the world.

But I also wanted to figure out who had done this, and why. And I realised that it was entirely possible that Chuck might be able to help me after all. I waved him back over, and put on my best conciliatory face.

"Look, I'm sorry," I said. "I'm being an arse. This is fucking stressful for everyone, I know."

He nodded, curtly. "Apology accepted."

"I was wondering... do you know where Mike Green is? I'd have expected him to be here – he's been hanging around all the time, so I'm quite surprised he hasn't shown up."

Chuck looked amused. "Haven't you heard? He's in the *Celebrity Big Brother* house. He went in yesterday!"

So either Green had got himself a truly impressive alibi, and had somehow managed to kill Jeffrey while locked in a house surrounded by TV cameras, or he was innocent and someone else was the killer. While I was not going to give up my suspicions completely, it did look like it might have been someone else.

"So what do you think will happen with the new album now? With Jeffrey not around to produce it, I mean?"

He smiled. "It'll be improved. I'm sorry Jeffrey's dead of course, and I'll pray for his soul, but he was a useless hack. I don't know why Robert thought he needed him, and I'm sure Robert can finish the album without him. Robert was using him as a crutch, but he's a genius and he can do it without him." He actually rubbed his hands together in anticipation. "This album is going to be the greatest thing ever!"

And at that point, the call came from Andy, "Five minutes until showtime!"

In Cillaworld, apparently, murder didn't stop the show from going ahead.

# Can the Can

I visited Robert in the studio the day after Jeffrey's murder. Well, I say "visited", but he spent the entire time in the vocal booth, pressing his headphones to his ears.

He looked absolutely shaken. As far as I knew, he'd only known Jeffrey for a few months, but it looked like the murder had hit him far harder than Graham's had. (Though thinking back, that was a little unfair of me – I didn't know what his baseline was like before Graham's death. Maybe he'd been an actual functioning human being then, for all I knew. I doubted it though.)

He was just staring blankly at his microphone, his mouth slightly open. I wondered if he was actually going to start drooling.

"Shall we go for a take?" Scott the engineer eventually asked, as it became apparent that Robert wasn't going to initiate anything himself.

"What? Oh... yeah, I suppose. What song are we doing right now?"

Scott looked at his screen. " 'The Spirit of You.'"

Robert muttered to himself. "Spirit of You... Spirit of You... Can I have a playback, Scott?"

Scott sighed and said "Sure." He pressed a button, and Robert started pressing his headphones to his ears. Scott clicked off the talkback so Robert couldn't hear him. "He's been like this for ages. Jeffrey used to be able to corral him a bit. He can't remember the songs at all."

Robert's voice came through. "Okay, I think I've got it."

"Okay," said Scott. "Take... twenty five."

He hit the playback button again, and Robert started singing. I couldn't hear the track he was singing along to, but whatever this was he was singing didn't make any musical sense at all to me. I looked over at Scott.

"Is this... is this meant to be what he's singing?"

Scott looked back, his face a model of weary resignation. "Fuck knows. It certainly doesn't fit the song at all. I mean, they say he's a musical genius, so maybe it's something clever and beyond me, but personally I'm coming to the conclusion that he's just a massive wanker who's not entirely sure where he is, or even who he is."

"Can I hear that back?" Robert said at the end.

"Sure thing," said Scott. "Want to come in here and listen?"

"No, just through the cans. There's more parts I want to track after this."

He was just overdubbing endless vocal harmonies over and over, not playing any new instrumental parts. He didn't seem to be making a record as much as just in a holding pattern. After an hour or so, he came into the control room for a coffee break, and I tried asking him about what he was planning to do now their outside producer was gone, but he just said "oh, we'll get it done" and seemed noncommittal about how.

Robert seemed very hesitant about this whole business of making a new album. All these vocal parts he was singing seemed to me to be just attempts at the same kind of part, but he wasn't multitracking or thickening them. It was just... aimless noodling, of a kind that didn't seem to fit the style of the tracks he was recording.

"Is this really what you want for these songs?" I asked him, wondering if he was actually trying to get work done at all.

"Oh, this is how I work," he replied. "You have to feel around, try new things, listen to what you've already done, and generally play about. Your best work always comes from noodling, not from trying to get it right first time."

"But doesn't the album have to be done by the end of the month?"

"Oh yeah, but it's the eighty twenty rule – you get eighty per cent of the work done in the last twenty per cent of the time. You have to feel around until it all comes together at the end."

"But isn't that the opposite of what Jeffrey was saying? That you have to have everything prepared in advance to get it done quickly?"

"Yeah, well, Jeffrey's dead."

He went back into the control booth and stood at the mic with his headphones on. "Okay, Scott," he said to the engineer through the speakers, "can I try that again?"

Scott, a thickset man who was chain-smoking thin rollup cigarettes in defiance of the laws against workplace smoking, sighed and pressed the talkback button. "Absolutely nothing would give me greater pleasure, Robert. I never, ever, get bored of hearing you sing the same part over and over again."

The music started again in Robert's headphones, but we couldn't hear it in the control room. "He doesn't pay me enough to listen to this shit" said Scott, in response to my quizzical look.

"Ooh, ooh, what'll she do now? Ooh ooh aaaah" came from the speakers, as Robert tried again to get the vocal part down.

"How was that, Scott?"

"Superlative as always, Robert." Scott clicked off the talkback again. "Fucking arsehole." I turned towards the doorway, heading for the toilet. "Make us a cup of tea, would you, love? Three sugars."

I glared at him. He looked confused for a second, and then shocked, as if he hadn't realised what he was doing.

"Oh, I'm sorry, I didn't mean that to come out like that. I wasn't asking you because you're a woman or anything like that. It's just that you were heading out that way – I have to concentrate on the job, and Robert's doing his vocals, or something that might seem the same as vocals in his head, wherever that is at the moment. You're here as a spectator, so you have a bit more freedom than I do, that's all I meant."

I softened slightly. I'd been judging him a little harshly, I realised, and most of it was frankly bigotry. He was a big white bloke, he wore a brown leather jacket, he smoked roll-ups and had an uneducated working-class accent and called me "love", so I'd been assuming he was a misogynist arse.

"Sure, I get it," I said. "I'll stick the kettle on."

I turned to go out to the kitchen. Just as I was on my way out of the door, I heard him say "And make us a sandwich while you're in there."

I whirled round, furiously, only to see him trying desperately not to burst out laughing. "I'm sorry, I just couldn't resist," he said, and I smiled, but inside I'd added him to my Enemies List. I don't like blokes who "jokingly" pretend to be sexist Neanderthals (side note, from what I can gather Neanderthals were actually perfectly nice people, and probably shouldn't be slurred against in that way, but they're not around any more and pigs are, and I try to keep my inaccurate slurs aimed at the dead). Blokes like that are all too likely to actually take the sandwich if you do make them one, and only say they're joking when you act like they're annoying you.

But I didn't particularly want a confrontation with Scott right now, so I pretended that I found him as hilarious as he evidently found himself, and went through to the kitchen.

I'd been in recording studios before, popping in occasionally to see Jane, and I'd got used to them over the years, and to the strange idiosyncracies of them (I'd been in more than one studio where they actually still had an Atari ST being used, because someone had got used to having one in the 90s and built their workflow around it – musicians are second only to writers in their unwillingness to adopt new technology). They tend to be much grimier, less glamorous, places than most people expect – they're all in old warehouse spaces on the edges of grey industrial estates, and have couches with the foam stuffing poking out of them.

In this case, the kitchen also doubled as an office, because space is at a premium in these places, and so opposite the fridge and kettle was a table with an old PC on it, and by it I noticed a couple of CD jewel cases. While I was waiting for the kettle to boil, I had a quick look at them. They were both cheap CDRs, and on the inlay of one was scrawled "Cillas rough mixes: Robert copy", and the other had "Cillas rough mixes: Jeff copy." I'm a compulsive fidgeter, so I opened the one saying "Jeff copy" and found it was empty.

I suddenly got a strange thought in my head – what if there was something about that music that had caused the deaths? What if the CD had been stolen for that reason? I had a look at the other CD case, the one saying "Robert copy", and saw that there was still a CD in there. I stuck it in my jacket pocket, thanking the Godess that I'd borrowed Jane's jacket and she was butch enough to have men's clothes with pockets.

The kettle boiled, I made tea for Scott and me and went back in.

# Ain't Ya Something Honey?

The next day, the band were playing in Leeds. At the soundcheck the band members were discussing tracks from the new album. Frankly I wasn't sure how they could even tell the songs apart, given that they were all pretty much the same kind of audio mush, but apparently they had opinions about them.

"Should we maybe do some of these in the show?" asked Terry. "You know, to promote the album?"

"Can we really pull that clean sound off live, though?" Pete replied. "I mean, it's all layers of synths and nylon guitar and tinkly shit. Can we really do that with guitars, bass, and drums?

"You know, I'm starting to quite enjoy that one 'Sunshine is Me'," said Terry, "and that one's mostly guitars, isn't it? We could probably do that." The other band members nodded cautiously. He continued. "I wouldn't have thought it was my sort of thing, but it turns out I really like the tune. Why don't we work that one up?"

"Which one's that again?" Sid asked.

"You know," said Pete, "do do do do... we were drinking wine/It was our time..."

"Why would we want to do that?" asked Robert. "No-one knows the song, no-one in the audience cares about anything but the hits anyway. Why make more work for ourselves?"

"Because it's fucking boring doing this job without at least changing up the setlist a bit," replied Terry. "We're spending the entire show just running through the same thing every time. If I wanted to do that I'd have got a factory job."

Yeah, like there are still factory jobs, I thought, but I wasn't going to get involved in the band's arguments – that wasn't my job.

"Oh, I'm sorry you're so bored going out in front of thousands of cheering people." Kate butted in. "You're talking about a song on an album that's only half recorded. We haven't even finished making the record yet, but you want to go out there and play this song in front of thousands of people with mobile phones? The song will be all over YouTube within ten minutes of you hitting the first note. And what if Robert decides to change the arrangement, or cut out the middle eight, or just drop the song altogether from the album? We end up with a rough draft all over the Internet, and what does that do to record sales?"

"What it does is promote the fucking album!" Pete said. "And if it's different from the finished version, all the better. What happens then is people say 'wow, if that's how good the outtakes are, how good is the album itself?'"

"Yeah, cause that worked so well with *Rising Up*, didn't it?" Robert said.

"Well, it would have, if... oh you know what? Forget it. You're right. You're the genius, after all. So enlighten us mere mortals, O great genius. at what point is it acceptable for us to start performing our new record live? When the audience have died from old age? Or just when they've died from boredom from us playing the same twenty songs every night without any variation at all?"

Terry interrupted. "I don't think we need to worry about the audience getting bored just yet. I mean, we've only done about five gigs, and they're excited just to see us again right now. We can worry about varying the set when we've proved ourselves live again a bit."

"So, decision?" asked Andy. "I need to know if we're going to be playing this one so I can prepare charts."

"We're not doing it" said Robert. "We don't need the hassle, simple as. I don't even see why we need to be practising. We're playing fine, aren't we? No need to wear the songs out by going over them over and over again. This is meant to just be a soundcheck, not a whole sodding rehearsal."

"We're playing fine *because* we keep rehearsing," said Pete. "We've only been playing together for five sodding minutes. We're not properly tight yet. The audiences can't tell that because they're excited, and because Andy and Simon are doing a fine job of covering for us..."

...and Jane, I thought. I was more than used to her contributions being erased by the blokes she was working for.

"But... Kate was talking about YouTube videos. I'll be fucking embarrassed when some of those performances start showing up on YouTube. We're okay, but we don't sound like a proper band yet, and that'll be very obvious to anyone listening to us sober in their own home, rather than in a crowd of fans at a gig."

And he didn't know the half of it, I realised. The band still didn't realise that Robert's guitar had got into the mix a couple of days earlier. Thank God that while they could talk about YouTube and so on, none of them actually knew how to work anything on the Internet, or this row would have been ten times as intense.

But it seemed odd to me that it was Robert, whose new song they were talking about playing, who didn't want to be playing it. Surely he'd want to do one of the new songs, especially since he'd made the recordings without any of the other band members' involvement?

"Look," Robert said, "I just want to get through the shows. That's all. Just turn up, play the set, and go home. I don't know why I'm here. I never liked being on stage anyway, and I'm only doing it to save your sorry arses."

"We didn't ask you to," said Pete. "And we all know why you don't want to learn the new songs. It's because you can't play the fuckers. There's no shame in admitting you're a tenth-rate musician and can barely hold your axe the right way up."

Robert's face started to redden.

"No, come on, we're all friends here," said Pete, continuing to needle the man he hated so much. "You can say it. Get it off your chest. Stand up proud and say 'I'm Robert Michaels, and I'm a no-talent shit who's scared to do anything new in case it reveals how useless I am to the public.' You can say it. We won't judge you."

"Oh for fuck's sake!" Robert shouted. "I don't need this shit. I'm off."

He took his guitar off and walked out. Pete went and sat at his drum kit, until the others turned and looked at him.

"Okay... I'll go and talk to him," he said.

# You Could Have Told Me

I followed Pete out, at a distance, to see what he could possibly say to Robert. He found Robert in a corridor near their dressing rooms. Surprisingly, without the rest of the band as an audience, Pete seemed far more friendly – almost tender, in fact. He walked up to Robert and put his arm round his shoulder, and I stood a few paces behind them as Pete spoke softly to Robert.

"Look, come back in. No-one's going to get pissed off at you if you just want to do the same shit we've been doing all along."

"So you're not going to tell them?"

"Of course I'm not going to fucking tell them. I'm not stupid. I remember very well what we agreed, and I know what you can do to me if I tell anyone at all. Your secret's safe."

"But how can I trust you?"

"I haven't told anyone in forty years, have I? I'm hardly going to start now. Just look at it logically. It's not like I could gain anything at all from it. It's not like *Goodbye Dragon* sold so many copies I'm going to start making massive royalties from it, is it?"

"It's the principle of the thing..."

At this point Pete's voice did start to rise slightly, and he removed his arm from Robert's shoulder. He turned to face him rather than standing side-on, and I could see his face. I think he actually made eye contact with me then, but he quickly looked back towards Robert. "Principle? You've got no fucking principles, and you know it. There's nothing you care about other than your own reputation."

Robert looked as if he'd been punched. Even though I couldn't see his face, I could see him physically tense up, and cringe, like a

137

dog that's seen a rolled-up newspaper coming towards its muzzle. "It was never about my reputation," he said. "You know that. I did it for..."

"Oh, spare me the rationalisations," Pete said. "You and I both know what went on. We know what you did to me, and we know what you did to Ray."

"Don't say his name."

"Guilty about something?"

"I'm... I never meant to..."

Pete sighed. "I know you didn't, and that's the problem. If you'd ever thought about anything we wouldn't be in this mess. But we are, and like it or not, we have to work together. Now, I know this is all difficult for you, but it's a fuck of a lot harder for me. But neither of us can change that, so let's just go back in there and run through 'Misty Lady' again, all right?"

"You're right. I know you're right. If I could change what happened back then..."

"Yeah, well you can't, can you?"

"I'd give anything to. I'd give my life to bring him back."

"Yeah, well." Pete said. "You can't, so let's just forget it, eh?"

"Yes. Yes, you're right. Thank you, Pete."

I was quite surprised to hear all this, not least because it was the longest, and most coherent, conversation I'd heard from Robert since he joined the tour.

"But at some point," Pete continued, "you'll have to relisten to those old records and at least learn the tunes of the songs. We can cope with you not knowing the words – Teleprompters exist for a reason, or you can even just write them on the back of your hand if you need to – but you need to have some idea of the tunes."

"Aye, you're right, fair enough," Robert said, his voice full of resignation. "Look, I'm sorry I'm being a bit of an arse. I wasn't prepared for any of this, and I don't really know how to cope with this situation at all."

"I don't want your apology, and you'll get no sympathy from me. This is a situation of your own making, and you'll have to figure out how to deal with it. But you're here now, and you're here to do a job. I don't expect you to pull your own weight – Christ knows you've never done that before – but you need to get it together enough that you don't fuck it up for the rest of us. All right?"

Robert nodded. "Look, Pete, I really am sorry. For everything, not just for this."

"Yeah, well that and two quid will get me a bag of chips. Look, I'm not going to do anything to harm your reputation as the perfect genius who's too beautiful for this world. I'm not going to reveal your secret and jeopardise the tour. I need this for my pension. But I'm not going to be your mate either, and I'm not twenty-one any more. I'm going to do my job, and I expect you to do your own."

"Fair enough," said Robert, glumly. "I suppose that's all I deserve."

"It's a fuck's sight better than you deserve," said Pete. "Anyway, let's get back in there and stagger them all with some more examples of your sparkling genius, eh?"

They went back into the rehearsal room, and shut the door behind them. A few seconds later I heard the muffled sounds of the riff of "John Paul's Art" come through the door.

And as the door shut, I saw that Chuck had been stood behind it. He'd heard the conversation as well. While I didn't particularly want to talk to the man, I decided that given that we'd both been essentially eavesdropping on the same thing, it would probably be an idea to compare notes, so I went over to him.

"What was all that about?" I asked him.

"I don't know," he replied thoughtfully. "That was really, really weird."

"You don't know?" I was surprised at the admission. "I thought you knew everything about this band. How could they have some forty-year-old secret you haven't found out?"

He looked like he was about to start crying, and I felt quite sorry for him. For a second I wanted to reach my arms out for a hug, but only a second. "I don't know!" he replied. "I... the more I get to know about this band, the more I start to wonder if I actually know anything at all about them. You know... I looked up to these people. I still do. I mean... they made the most beautiful music I've ever heard. But they're such... such assholes!"

Takes one to know one, I thought, but all I said was "I know what you mean. Bunch of massive egos, based on so little."

He looked affronted. "No, it's not based on little. If anyone deserves to have an ego, it's them. I just... I wish they could be more graceful about it, you know?"

I had to agree with Mr. Lack Of Self-Awareness 2018 there. He was, for once, talking a lot of sense.

"I sometimes think..." he trailed off.

"No, go on."

"No, nothing. I just wish that people could ever live up to the mental image you have of them."

"Never meet your heroes," I said.

"It's worse than that," he replied. "I'm starting to wonder who my heroes actually are at all. I mean... that man there, that can't be the man who wrote *Goodbye Dragon* and *Rising Up*, can it? How could he... how could it be him who wrote those albums?"

I shrugged. "He's an acid casualty. They get like that. His brain was probably working forty years ago."

Chuck looked at me oddly for a second. "No... I mean..." he shook his head. "Never mind, forget I said anything, You obviously don't understand, and that's probably for the best."

We went back inside.

# 20th Century Boy

At this point, I was going to have to get some actual interview quotes. I was having to generate so much material on this tour that I'd probably end up turning it into a book anyway, so my thought was to get a few in-depth interviews that I could excerpt for a piece for *Rolling Stone* or *Mojo* and then also mine for information for the book.

Terry had seemed by far the most approachable of the actual band members, and he was the one who'd originally formed the band, so I decided that I was going to ask him for the first interview proper. We'd talked earlier, of course, for general background, but this was going to be an on-the-record thing with notepad and tape recorder (or at least with my phone recording everything). He agreed readily, even eagerly. I suspect, thinking about it now, that he'd not have had very many interview requests.

Once again we were sat in an old-man pub. Terry seemed to spend all day every day in a Wetherspoons or nearest equivalent, nursing pints of bad lager until the time came to turn up for the sound-check. I sat down in a booth with him and stuck my phone on one of the less-sticky bits of the table, to record what he said.

"No-one ever wants to talk to the bass player," he told me. "People don't even really know what the bass is. They know what the drums, guitar, and vocals are, but more people than you'd think just think the bass is another guitar that's not doing anything interesting like the bloke up front who gets to go tweedly tweedly dee with his one. Unless you're also the singer, like Sting or Paul McCartney or someone, I suppose."

I nodded. "It's very much a background job, isn't it? How did you end up being the bass player?"

"Well, it's very simple," he smiled. "I wanted to form a band, but I couldn't play anything. I was the singer, but then Graham came in and I had to find an instrument. Drums are bloody difficult, and Ray and Rob already played guitar, and basses only have four strings... honestly, for the first year or so I was only playing root notes on open strings for most of it. I had a good sense of rhythm, but wasn't playing much in the way of a melody."

We talked about the three or four early hits he'd played on, and I asked him his opinion of them, but he didn't seem particularly interested in talking about them in any detail.

"There are a couple of bits I'm proud of, like that riff in 'Rumble Rabble.' But for the most part I just played the songs, you know? I was never the world's best bass player. You know, I'm having more fun on this tour playing the stuff I wasn't on than the stuff they did when I was still in the band. I just wish we were doing more tracks from *Goodbye Dragon*. We're basically ignoring that album, but it's the best thing they ever did. Always been a favourite of mine."

"I'm surprised you listened to their stuff after they kicked you out. Wouldn't that be a bit painful?"

"Aye, it was at first, no question about it. I mean, they were my mates, you know? – well, except for Graham. Clive brought him in, and I never liked the man. I'm fairly convinced it was him who pushed for them to kick me out. He never liked that I was getting all the girls. Anyway. It did hurt hearing their records after I was kicked out, at first, but you couldn't really avoid hearing them on the radio back then, and frankly some of them were bloody good.

"But I didn't buy any until *Goodbye Dragon*. I felt so awful when Ray died – and also a bit of 'there but for the grace of God', you know? I mean, if they hadn't kicked me out, maybe I'd have gone the same way, or instead of him. So I bought that album... I don't know. I've never put it into words until right now. But the other Cillas were the only people I'd shared Ray's friendship with, so I wanted to reconnect with them and mourn with them, and by buying that album I felt like I was doing that."

I nodded. I got exactly what he meant, sadly enough.

"So in a way it was what they call closure now, I suppose. Hearing Graham and Robert sing all those gorgeous songs about me dead mate Ray. But at the same time... I'd always thought Ray was probably the talent in that songwriting pair – he was the better musician, and he just seemed more *alive* than Robert – but those new songs of Robert's were so good, it just made me think 'You poor sod, Ray, they didn't need you any more than they needed me, but at least I'm alive to realise it.'

"It's amazing, really. We'd all thought that Ray was the real talent, when I was in the band, but I picked up that *Goodbye Dragon* record, and... shit, it was better than anything we'd done while I was in the Cillas. Absolutely no question about that. It seemed like Ray had been holding Rob back, rather than anything else. I mean, that album had some fucking beautiful stuff in it."

"You thought Ray was the talent until then? That's really fascinating – everyone talks about Robert as the genius. How exactly did Ray and Robert's writing partnership work?"

"Oh, we never knew. They'd just bring us the songs together, when they'd finished them. We never got involved with the writing. Usually the first we'd hear of it would be Ray and Rob sat in the studio, Ray strumming through it on his guitar while Rob sang it to us. Then we'd learn the chords and do a run-through of the basic rhythm track, and Ray, Rob, and Gray would do the rest later."

"How do you mean, do the rest later?"

"Well, they did most of the vocal parts between the three of them. We'd sing the parts live, of course, but they were mostly overdubbed by those three. And obviously Ray would put his lead guitar parts down on a separate track. What always surprised me was that so would Rob. He'd lay down the rhythm or piano parts by himself, without the rest of the band around. I always felt a little bit hurt by that, in a way – they were meant to be our records, not just by those three with me and Dave acting as session musicians. Of course, it turned out that was exactly how they saw us, and they got rid of us the first chance they had. That's one thing I'll say for Ray, actually – he may well have been dead weight in the songwriting department, but he at least had the decency to say he was sorry when we got kicked out. That's more than Graham or Robert ever did; even to this day neither of them has apologised, and of course now Graham never will."

He sighed. "I'm sorry, love. This is probably no good for your booklet stuff, is it? Tell you what, just make some shit up and stick my name on it. No-one'll know any different, and I'll be happy to say it was me. Call it a tribute to Ray, getting credit for holding you back."

He swigged down the rest of his lager, stood up, and left.

# My Oh My

I realised something – everyone had been talking about this band's music, but I really didn't know anything other than the hits they'd been playing live. Yet whether it was cool kids like Beth and Claire, or a gargantuan wanker with bad breath like Chuck, they were all going on specifically about this album *Goodbye Dragon*, which didn't have any of those hits on. If I was going to write about this band, I'd have to at least listen to that so I could talk intelligently about it.

I looked it up on Spotify, and there were something like ten different versions of it, labelled stuff like "Deluxe Edition" and "2-CD version" and "2012 Remastered Version" and all sorts like that. Bloke record, I decided. A record very specifically for middle-aged blokes who spend a hundred quid a week on buying the same record they've already got. Men who buy gold cables for their stereos and call themselves audiophiles.

But, not all records those men like are dreadful. As many as three percent of them actually have a good song on. And anyway, I wasn't listening to the music for my own enjoyment, but to understand it for work. So I picked the version with the fewest tracks, which I guessed meant it was the proper album, and turned on my speakers.

It'd been told it was an album you should listen to in the dark (they always say that about that kind of record) so I put the album on, and lay back, closed my eyes, and waited to see what all the fuss was about.

The first few notes were utterly unlike anything I'd heard from the band before, other than that one song "Catch and Return" they'd played a couple of times. There was a cello and some sort of high brass instrument (Jane later told me it was a piccolo trumpet), and then Robert's voice came in, whisper-singing rather than that screech he'd used so effectively on the hits.

"And so it's time to part, it seems, but I shall see you in my dreams, remember..."

The words weren't great – they seemed sort of juvenile, to be honest – but they fit the music perfectly. Writing about music isn't my thing, and I don't really have a vocabulary for it, but this music seemed spectral. It wasn't just unlike everything else the Cillas had done, it was unlike everything I'd heard.

Part of it definitely reminded me of some of the classical music I'd heard – there was a definite resemblance to some of Bach's stuff, though I only know the famous bits of his work – but some of it sounded almost mariachi or something. It felt like religious music, but it wasn't in the style of the hymns we used to sing at school, where every line would end with a long note so the people who'd got lost and were "da-da-da "ing through the tune could find their place again.

The thing that was surprising was how utterly different from the Cillas' other stuff this was. While the melodies for their early hits were quite flat – even I can sing along with them, and I've got about the range of a cat that's being strangled – this was all over the place. The notes were falling unpredictably, but at the same time they all made perfect sense as soon as you heard them. Yes, that was the only possible note that could go there, even though there was no way you could have predicted it from the notes before.

And it sounded so empty. The record seemed to be just the echoes of music, like if you'd found some way to extract the song and just leave the reverb. It was a glorious, marvellous, emptiness, though – one that inspired the same kind of awe as watching 2001 or gazing at Stonehenge – an astonishment that humans could do this.

Graham's voice was on there, of course, but he was even more echoey and in the background than everything else. Sometimes he was singing something that could technically be described as a lead vocal part, but even there Robert's "backing vocals" seemed to dominate somehow. This was a gorgeous, empty, piece of minimalism and there was no place in it for a cock-rocking frontman. It was more of a mournful whisper than a yell of lust.

And Pete's vocals were all over it too – sometimes doubling Robert, sometimes doubling Graham, and sometimes off doing his own thing.

If Pete had spent as much time in the studio with Robert as I'd been told, that made sense – Sid and Pete were both excellent singers even now, and while Sid wasn't really on the album much other than his guitar playing, Pete had spent those long months in the studio with Robert. If he'd had nothing else to do other than play the drums, support Robert and sing, it made sense for him to have done a lot of singing.

It made me wonder what exactly had happened to cause the split between the two men – they seemed to be in harmony on the album in both the literal and metaphorical senses – and I wondered again about how all this fed into the murders, but I decided not to let myself get sidetracked in that way. I was going to pay attention to this music.

I was beginning to see why people like Chuck described Robert as a genius. Why had he never made any music that sounded like this before, and why didn't he make any music that sounded like it after this? I mean, people grow and change, so I can see how he could have made a massive leap in his ability, but when you've levelled up like that, surely you'd carry on making music?

Why weren't there a dozen more albums of this stuff? This couldn't be a fluke – this was craftsmanship, not the accidental magnificence you sometimes get from an artist who chances on something brilliant but doesn't know what they've done. I know all about the latter, of course, and I've learned to tell the difference from a mile off. This was deliberate.

Of course, the record had been made in the wake of a friend's death, and maybe it would take that level of emotional intensity to spur Robert into making such heartfelt music – but once you've got that level of ability to do something, you can do good work, even if not great work, without inspiration. I'm nowhere near as good as a writer as Robert was as a songwriter, but I was more than able to write decent work without being inspired at all – one of the dirty secrets of the creative industries is that there's relatively little creativity to them in the way most people think of the word. You just do the graft, you make up for lack of inspiration with technique, and this album was full of technique.

So where had Robert's technique all gone? Yes, he was an acid casualty now, but he wasn't completely lacking in brain function. How could he have created this and yet be so useless now?

I decided I needed to talk to someone about the band history behind this album. Much as I dreaded the thought, I was going to have to speak to Chuck.

# Bend Over Beethoven

I collared Chuck the next day in the break between the soundcheck and the show, while the band were off doing the meet-and-greet sessions, at which people who'd paid a hundred quid a head got to stand in a line, attempt to make eye contact with them, and get a photo taken on their phones.

I'd rather have talked to Beth and Claire about what had been going on in the band, but I knew they weren't coming to this show, as Glasgow was too much of a trek for them, and I wanted to get some information today, while the album was fresh in my memory.

Luckily, I knew the way to get information out of Chuck. He was a man who had a massive amount of contempt for women, and so the best way to get him to talk was to get him to mansplain. I pretended ignorance, and he opened right up.

"Chuck, could you explain what happened with *Goodbye Dragon*? I mean, I've heard all the hits and so on, but this *Goodbye Dragon* thing is different. All those big hits are the same – they're all stampy, stompy guitar-riff songs about fancying someone who doesn't fancy you – all teen angst and testosterone. But *Goodbye Dragon* barely has any guitars on it, and it's all about loss and death. It's this sort of orchestral song cycle thing. How do you go from one to the other – it's like it's not even the same band."

He looked thoughtful. "Well, really, of course, it wasn't. Most of that album was just Pete and Robert playing together. The others weren't really involved with it. It's basically a Robert Michaels solo album, with Pete on drums. Which is why it's so much better than the other ones."

"So it was just those two on the album?"

"Yeah, for most of it. The band were all absolutely devastated by Ray's death, of course. Sid didn't want to continue for a while, and he switched to lead guitar, so he spent those months basically practising the old parts Ray had played, so he could reproduce them on stage. And Graham never played on the backing tracks anyway. So Robert and Pete were in the studio for months laying down tracks, and then Sid and Graham came in to do a few overdubs at the end."

"And they were okay with that?"

"Oh yes, they were both more about the live performance than they were about the recordings. And remember that Sid wasn't even a full member of the band, so he wouldn't get any more money from working harder on it. He was only on a salary."

"Doesn't that apply to Pete as well? Why would he have spent so much time working on the album, if he wasn't going to get paid more?"

He thought. "You see, that's the funny thing about Pete. Did you know he was a bit of a Robert Michaels fanboy?"

I was shocked. "Pete?! Pete who can't go five minutes without having a go at Robert? That Pete?"

"Oh yes. He joined the band because he was obsessed with them. Considered Robert a genius – rightly, of course – and he just wanted to bask in the presence. He was living the fans' dream – he was just happy to be working with the great Robert Michaels in the studio."

"So what happened?"

"Well, nobody knows, except that something went wrong between them during the recording of *Rising Up*. That was going to be the album that would make *Goodbye Dragon* sound like some three-year-old kid's recorder practise, by all accounts. They were making it in downtime during the *Goodbye Dragon* tour, and the bootlegs of what was done are just astounding. But then, just after *Goodbye Dragon* actually came out, Pete just quit the band. There was apparently some legal shit between him and Robert, and the band just splintered. I always thought they should at least have finished *Rising Up*, but they just sort of gave up."

"Do you know why he quit?"

"No. In fact... I don't even know if he quit or he was fired. They got in another drummer to finish off the tour, halfway through – it was that sudden. Kenney Jones from the Small Faces, before he went off to join the Who of course. I've got some audience recordings of those shows – they're great, but Kenney didn't have the feel for the songs that Pete or Dave did. I always wondered what they'd have sounded like if they'd carried on with him, but we'll never know. One of the great missed opportunities."

Chuck seemed always to talk in these big paragraphs full of long sentences – I supposed he wasn't used to getting interrupted. I could see why he put out so many podcasts – the man could easily talk for hours on end if you wound him up and got him going on about the Cillas.

"So this other album they were working on..."

"*Rising Up*."

"*Rising Up*, yes. Did Robert not want to put those songs out as a solo album or something?"

"That's the odd thing. He just completely gave up songwriting al-together. Became a recluse. He literally didn't record or release one note of music between the end of the *Goodbye Dragon* tour and the start of the sessions for this one."

"You're sure he never recorded anything at all? Not in a home studio, not just for himself? For forty years he didn't play or record at all?"

"Yeah. I mean, it surprises everyone when they find out. But it's a fact. I once tracked him down for an interview with my fanzine, about fifteen years ago, and he just wouldn't talk – I mean, he threatened to call the police on me – but he told me he'd pawned his guitar the week the tour ended, and he'd never bought another one. And... it checks out. I've asked all the experts – Andrew Ledgely, Ken Poynton, John Spilsbury – and they've all said exactly the same thing. He sold his guitar, never played again, never wrote a song again. He stayed involved in the business side of the Cillas' company, making sure the catalogue was properly exploited, licensing the songs out for films, that sort of thing. But he refused to get involved in any of the musical side of it at all. He wouldn't go into the studio when Ledgely was auditioning tapes for the reissue programme, he wouldn't let them use any of his old demos, he wasn't involved in the remixes... it's like he just gave up even thinking about music at all until this tour started. It's honestly a miracle that he's doing this."

"No wonder the new songs sound different."

He looked confused. "What do you mean?"

"The new songs. You know... the ones they've been working on recently. They sound so bland compared to *Goodbye Dragon*, but I suppose if you've not written a song for forty years you'll lose the knack."

"Yes, well, that's down to Jeffrey Washington, of course. Thank God he's gone. Now Robert's true abilities in the studio will shine."

"But... the songs will be the same, won't they? And they still don't sound like the old material."

He looked thoughtful. "No... no I suppose they won't."

At that point the band came back into the backstage area, and Chuck went off to schmooze, leaving me none the wiser.

# Teenage Rampage

When you're touring the country with a bunch of men – even when the tour is the kind of laid-back affair where there are a couple of days between shows, so you get to go back home on occasion and you're not spending all day cooped up in a bus – there are a few things you start to miss, and one of them is female company.

Other than Jane and myself, there weren't many women in the organisation. The sound engineer was a woman, and obviously there were Janine and Kate, but those two didn't spend much time on the road. But the rest of the band were blokes, and so were most of the crew – the road life attracts a certain kind of burly bloke who wears promotional T-shirts from beer companies, and who enjoys lugging heavy electrical items around.

And so we'd ended up getting quite close to Beth and Claire, the two young fans I'd met early on. Just because they were faces we kept seeing, and they were women from roughly our own generation (I'm technically a Millennial, as is Jane, while they were eight or nine years younger than me, so part of some generation that hadn't yet been given an annoying demographic name), we'd ended up gravitating to them.

I liked them a lot more than most of the blokefans we'd see at the same venues. They were witty, and they were appropriately cynical about the flaws of their idols, and so when there was a day free in Birmingham before the show (we'd got in the day before, and sound-check wasn't until 6PM) and they'd let us know they were in town, we decided to go out for a drink together.

(We'd at first talked about going for a meal, but it turned out that Beth had dietary stuff that clashed with my veganism, and we couldn't find anywhere where we could be sure we could both eat, especially in a city none of us were familiar with. But everyone could at least drink a glass of red wine.)

So, we were sat in a pub in the middle of a Tuesday afternoon, and it was pleasingly empty. It was one of those pubs that's pretty much entirely brown, and which has a flatscreen TV in every corner tuned to a sports channel, but with the sound turned off. There was one bored bar worker, stood behind the bar cleaning glasses, but we had the place to ourselves otherwise, and it was nice just to tune out and relax with some friends.

"So, how did you two meet up?" Beth asked us. "I mean, you don't seem to have very much in common... no offence but..." she looked flustered for a second, but Jane and I both laughed.

"We don't really," I said. "We don't share a lot of the same interests – Jane's a music person, obviously, while I'm really more into films and computers. She's a cat person, and I love dogs. We both have the same politics, but that's about it."

Jane nodded. "But we both grew up in the same tiny little shithole town, and it wasn't as if there was much in the way of queer nightlife there, and we sort of found each other. Then we reconnected at University, and... well..." as so often, Jane became nonverbal, and I took over.

"If you share the same experiences, that can make you feel comfortable around each other even if you don't have much in common in the conventional sense. And that feeling comfortable around each other... well, that's ninety percent of what we mean by love anyway."

Jane nodded, and appeared to have found her voice. "And as for the other ten percent, we... we think the same way. We finish each other's..."

"Derek," I interrupted, and she laughed. The other two smiled, in that way you do when other people are making a joke you don't get.

"Sorry," I said, "private joke. Reference to a TV thing. Carry on, Jane."

"No, I was finished," she said. "I was mostly just setting you up for the Derek line."

I smiled.

"So, you two," I said, "what do you actually do when you're not following the Cillas around?"

"I don't do much at all," said Beth. "I got some compensation after a botched surgery a few years back, and so I don't need to work."

I must have looked flustered – I couldn't think of which of the half-dozen different responses that came to mind would be appropriate – as Claire chipped in. "And I work in a bookshop."

She named a major chain which I'm not going to name, as I want them to stock this book, and I said "Oh, I'm sorry."

Jane looked confused. "Why are you sorry?"

"You know Rebecca? They sacked her when she went on sick leave after getting transphobic abuse from customers. And Dave's had to take them to an employment tribunal after they accused him of stealing with no evidence. The horror stories I've heard about them..."

Claire nodded. "They're arseholes. But it's a wage."

"Speaking of arseholes," said Beth, "is Chuck still hanging round stinking the place up?"

I nodded.

"See, this is why I'm getting out of this fandom," said Claire. "People like him."

"You're leaving the fandom?" I asked. I was rather horrified. She was, after all, someone who'd put a big part of her life into the band.

"Yeah," she said. "I've been thinking about it for a while. It's no fun any more. It's all men wanting to score points and suck up to the band members. Ever since the fandom moved away from Instagram and onto Facebook it's been colonised by boring men. And of course, with Graham dying and everything..."

"Also," Beth said, "Chuck's been poisoning the rest of the fandom against us. Said we were sleeping with Graham."

"The cheeky fucker!" I was horrified.

"It's his standard MO," Claire said. "Weasel his way in, and then smear anyone else who might threaten his status. Not really sure how he reconciles that with his religion, but he manages somehow."

I had a sip of the rather bitter Shiraz I was drinking, and decided I should probably raise the subject that had been going unspoken between all of us.

"So, these murders... who do you think did them?"

"Chuck. Definitely Chuck," Beth said, and we all burst out laughing.

"Seriously, though," she said, once the laughter had died down, "if you want my guess, it's Kate Michaels. Get Graham out of the way so Robert rejoins the tour, get Jeffrey out of the way so Robert can get more credit for the record. Also, she hates Janine Stewart, and she'd have happily killed Graham just to piss her off because she couldn't dance in the show any more."

"I'd guess Pete," Claire said. "Killed Graham because he wanted to get Robert back into the band because of that weird love/hate attraction/repulsion bromance thing they've got going on, then killed Jeffrey because Pete wasn't happy about being sidelined from the new album."

"So neither of you have a clue then?" I asked. They both shook their heads, deadpan, and we all burst out laughing.

"We shouldn't laugh about this," said Jane eventually. "It's an awful situation."

"You've got to laugh about this sort of thing," I said. "Got to show Death you're not scared of him. Give the bastard a bloody nose."

"Does Death have a nose?" asked Jane. "I mean, he's just got a skull. Could his skellington face even have a nosebleed?"

And the conversation continued along those intellectual lines for much of the rest of the afternoon.

# Alexander Graham Bell

Robert hadn't turned up for the show. This was a disaster, and the backstage area at the Birmingham venue was full of extremely angry musicians.

"What can we do?" Pete asked, frantically. "We can't go on without him. Is he answering his phone yet?"

"No," said Sid, who was pacing the floor, redialling over and over again trying to get through to him. "And Kate's not answering hers either. This is a fucking nightmare. We're on in ten minutes!"

"What's the problem?" Terry asked. "Look, he hardly does anything on stage anyway, and we all knew he was a complete flake before the tour started. Andy ghosts half his lead vocals anyway, we'll just get him to sing all of them. At least this way we won't have the problem of the lead singer's mouth not moving in time with his voice."

"The problem," Pete said, "is that this audience are there to see the legendary wonderful fantastical reclusive genius and his three side-kicks. You know and I know that Robert is dead weight, but the punters don't. As far as they're concerned, they're here to bask in the presence of genius, and you can't do that when you know it's Andy you're listening to. No offence, Andy."

"None taken, mate," Andy said. He seemed the only calm person in the room, and he was methodically going through his printed-out setlists making annotations. He looked up. "Okay, we need to decide, does the show go on tonight without him?"

Pete thought. "We can't, can we?"

"I've had this happen before," said Andy. "I was touring with The Electric Sprocket. San Francisco garage band from the 60s, same kind of deal as here."

157

"Oh yeah, I remember them!" Terry chipped in. "'Pathway to Your Mind's Eye,' right? I love that one."

"Yeah, that was them," Andy said. "Anyway, this was in 04 or 05. We were meant to be doing a UK tour, but their lead singer wouldn't get on the plane, and the others didn't find out until half way across the Atlantic. Apparently his numerologist advised him to only travel West, so he went for a holiday in Hawaii and didn't tell any of us. What we ended up doing was telling the audiences we'd refund half the ticket money if they stayed and watched the rest of us, or all the money if they wanted to leave. Almost all of them stayed."

"Why refund half the money, though?" Asked Terry.

"Because that way they stayed and didn't boo, and it was cheaper than refunding all of it. Now personally I don't care if we go on or not – I'm on a salary here and I get paid either way. And I know you're all on salaries too, but the band's reputation is your career, so it probably matters to you. Are we doing this, or can I get changed out of my stage suit?"

"Still no answer from Robert" said Sid, "but I say we do it."

"Okay, I'm in," said Terry. "What's the legal situation? We can't just give away the promoters' money, and what does the contract say?"

"Well since Kate's the co-promoter, and we can't get her, we'd better at least get Janine to sign off on the idea," said Pete, "I'll call her while you keep trying Robert and Kate." He paused for a second. "Christ, this is completely fucked. I'm going out to get some air. I'll let you know if I get an answer from her."

He walked out, his phone clutched to his ear.

Mike Green, who had come back from his time in the *Celebrity Big Brother* house and was once again a fixture of the tour, decided that what was needed more than anything was for him to bring his ego into it. "Do you want me to cover for him?"

Pretty much everyone in the room turned to him simultaneously and asked some variant of "what?" or "what the fuck?"

"No, I'm serious," he said. "They want a celebrity, I'm a celebrity." Nobody disillusioned him, so he continued. "I play guitar, I know the songs, it'd be something to take their minds off Robert not being there."

They all looked at him, and there was silence for a couple of beats, before Andy said, in an embarrassed tone of voice "So anyway, I can cover Robert's parts," (I managed not to snigger at the double entendre here, which I think was very mature of me) "but what do you want me to say? Are we going to say he's ill, or stuck in traffic, or what?"

"*I* don't fucking know," said Terry, who was at this point the only band member not trying to phone someone who wasn't answering. "I'm past the point where I give a shit about any of this. I just want to go out on stage, play me part, finish the tour, and never think about the fucking Cillas or Robert fucking Michaels ever again."

There were sympathetic nods from Andy, Simon, and Jane, all of whom had had their fill of the band's lack of professionalism.

"Look," Terry said, "say what you want. We've only got a few more days on the tour anyway, and they know we need you in order to function, Andy. They're not going to sack you this close to the end of the tour, and no-one wants to do another one, so just do what you have to do to let us get through the tour."

Andy nodded, and went back to annotating his setlist. He looked up a few seconds later. "Okay, we're going to drop 'Lilac Rainbow' from the set, because we don't have time to rearrange the harmony lines and that won't work without Robert, but we can do the rest. Everyone okay?"

Simon, Jane, and Terry all nodded and Sid waved from the corner of the room, where he was standing with his phone, redialling over and over to try to find out what was happening.

The stage manager came in. "Five minutes," she said, and then left again.

Sid, Terry, and Andy all picked up their guitars, and Simon his drumsticks, and moved towards the door leading to the stage. "Someone going to get Pete?" Terry asked.

"No need," said Jane, nodding towards the outside door, which Pete was coming through.

"Any joy, Pete?" Sid asked. "You get through to Janine?"

Pete's face looked ashen.

"Yeah. Yeah, I got through to her all right. She was with Kate." He paused, and I don't want to speak for the others, but I still feel sure we all knew what was coming. "Robert's dead. He's been murdered."

We all stood there in silence, and then Andy said "Well, I'd better get out of my stage suit then."

# The Tears I Cried

How could this have happened? A third person had now been killed, and still there was no way of knowing who had been doing it or why. I was beginning to envy the psychological profilers in stuff like Hannibal who can just look at a crime scene and say "ah, yes, this is my design. I am committing murders because I'm four foot ten and have a club foot, and an X in my name, and I was born on a Friday."

All I was able to do was think Oh my God, oh my God, people keep dying and that's horrible. Robert's dead! I mean, he's dead! Wiped from existence! He'll never be a sarcastic arse to Terry or Pete again! Never! And that's going to happen to all of us one day – maybe I should just curl into a little ball and cry forever.

This is not, as you might imagine, a thought process that's conducive to solving crimes, or even to the most basic functioning. Because this is one thing that those detective books don't tell you – it's fucking traumatic as all shit to have people keep getting murdered around you. Assuming I got out of this alive, I was going to be in therapy forever.

But this was a harder death than the other two we'd dealt with on the tour. I'd only met Graham and Jeffrey a couple of times each, and I'd not spent enough time with them to really be affected by their death. But Robert, even though he'd been standoffish and we hadn't talked the way I'd had proper talks with Terry or Pete, I'd spent much of the last few weeks in his presence. And even though I didn't know him well, I felt like I knew him, because everything everyone else in or around the band did revolved around him.

It was weird, really. He seemed like such an absence of a man, but everyone was affected by him anyway. I remembered reading about dark matter on some link I'd clicked through from Slashdot. Dark matter is stuff that we know must be in the universe, but we can't see it or understand it or measure it in any way. We only know it exists at all because of the way it distorts everything else in the universe. It affects everything, even though it doesn't seem to be there at all.

And Robert was very much like that. He was a vacant nonentity half the time, and the other half the time he was like a robot copy of a car salesman, going through the motions of acting like a normal person, but as if he was reading from a script. The only times I'd seen him be even vaguely human were in his clashes with Pete, but other than that, he was just... sort of there.

And yet... he was still a person, and he was still dead. And, astonishingly, I found that I missed him.

The show hadn't gone ahead, of course – even if anyone had been able to face going on stage, the audience wouldn't have been in the mood to have a fun night out right after being told that their idol had died – and so we'd all made our way to the same pub Jane and I had been in with Beth and Claire earlier. There weren't many of us – Greeny Green decided he had better things to do than hang around now the celebrity member of the band was dead – but Jane, Pete, Sid, Simon, Andy, Terry, Beth, Claire and I all sat around doing shots and reminiscing about Robert.

"He was an arse," said Pete, "but he didn't deserve that."

The band all nodded.

"What was your beef with him anyway?" Trevor asked. "You never did say."

Pete shook his head, took another drink, and leaned on the table with his glass in his hand. "Still can't say. Legal shit. But it's in the past."

"I'll drink to him," said Sid. "Hope he's up there in heaven with Graham and Ray right now."

Pete shook his head again. "Graham's a Mormon. He won't be in the same heaven as the other two."

"So do Mormons get their own special heaven then?" Sid asked.

Pete nodded. "Yeah. They say that everyone goes to heaven, but there are like... loads of heavens. And only Mormons go to the best one. That's why they have those magic underpants. To show they can go in there."

"Really?" Sid asked.

"He's right," I said. "There are, like, three heavens according to the Mormons. There's a top one for the Mormons, a bottom one for all the hopeless sinners like me, and a medium one for all the boring straight men like you lot."

"I'm gay!" said Simon, pretending to be outraged.

"Okay," I said, "then you can come to sinner heaven with me. But this lot," I waved my hand, nearly knocking a couple of glasses over, "they're all going to medium heaven."

"Actually, that's a point," said Trevor, "Ray was gay, too, wasn't he? So he'd be in bottom heaven. That's a thought, isn't it? A Cilla in every Heaven. Still, I suppose that means we'll all know someone up there, whichever heaven we end up in."

He raised his glass and looked skywards. "To Robert, thanks for keeping our place in Medium Heaven, mate." He took a swig, and the rest of us raised our glasses and said "to Robert."

After a lot of depressed chatter, and more than a few tears (astonishingly, Pete cried as much as anyone), someone finally brought up the future of the band. It was Trevor who finally said it.

"So... do we continue the tour or what? And how about the album?"

The others looked guilty, as if they'd all been wondering the same thing but not wanting to say it.

Pete eventually said "Look, we can't go out there tomorrow and be a party band, but..." he sighed. "I think, in the end, it depends on what Janine and Kate say, but my instinct is we reschedule the rest of the tour and then do it. It's a fucking horrible thing to say about someone who just died, but I think the tour will be easier without Robert, "

The others nodded. "But what about the album?" Sid said.

"What about it?" Pete asked. "Have any of us even heard the fucking thing? Is there even an album there? Do any of you know what stage it got to before Jeffrey carked it?"

The others shook their heads.

"Then I say we don't worry about that. We got the advance already, we're not even on the fucker much, and none of us have a copy. somebody else's problem."

He was right, or nearly right. Because one of us did have a copy. And I realised that I really should listen to mine.

# Rock Bottom

I left Jane in the pub – I didn't want to tell her what I was doing, and didn't want her to have to hear the voice of a dead colleague, so I headed back to the hotel room, saying I had a migraine.

If none of the band had a copy of the new album, that told me something rather worrying about it. I'd picked up Robert's copy, and Jeff's had been taken out of its case. I'd worried that it might be connected with the murder, and now with Robert dead, the only two people who had heard the album were gone. I needed to hear what was on that record, so I could make sure it had nothing to do with the killings.

I got back to the hotel room, and rooted through my bags. I'd stuck the CD in one of the cases, because I'd planned to listen to it on this trip anyway – this just made it more urgent. I eventually found it, and shoved it into the CD tray in my laptop, thanking Graham's Mormon God (for variety) for my continued insistence that my machines be able to play physical media (I spent enough time working in computer security that I won't trust "the cloud" with anything at all). I started up VLC, and played the CD.

It was... it was fucking awful. And it sounded nothing like the Cillas.

If I'd thought there was no continuity between the early hits and *Goodbye Dragon*, that was ten times as true here. I didn't want to speak ill of someone who'd just been killed, but just as miraculously as Robert had gained his talent for that album, he'd lost it for this one.

The music was bland, generic pap. There was no harmonic or melodic interest, the lyrics were trite, there was no emotion to it. It was as if someone had been given a brief of coming up with the most innocuous, dull music ever written, and had managed to do just that.

It was really weird hearing this from someone who had died that day. Normally, when you're reading or listening to the work of someone who'd died, there's this strange feeling of human connection and of opportunities missed – you think about that person, no longer there, making the thing you're enjoying. But in this case, there was nothing at all. There was no sense there that this music had been created by a human being with goals, aspirations, fantasies – this was like it had come out of a machine, with no contact with a human being at any point in the creative process.

I didn't know what to think about that. Was it just that I didn't like Robert and was trying to avoid whatever bits of his personality were coming through? I didn't think so, because I'd genuinely loved *Goodbye Dragon* when I'd heard it, and I'd already been aware the man was a complete dick. Or was it something else – was I avoiding hearing whatever clues were there in case they pointed to someone I did care about? I couldn't imagine that that was the case either.

But this music was... it was just nothingness. In a way that made sense – hadn't I just been thinking the same about Robert himself? Was this the musical equivalent of a used-car salesman? – but in another it made things more confusing. Robert seemed like a nothing because he was so enigmatic, so closed in on himself. This, on the other hand, seemed to just slide off your ears with its slickness and substancelessness.

I listened through the CD three times – it was only short, half an hour or so – before Jane got back to the room. I tried making notes about it. It had Robert's voice, of course, but the backing music was all close-mic'd nylon-string guitars, tinkling cymbals, and nineties drum sounds. It all sounded like Radio 2, right down to some horrendous autotune that had been slapped onto the vocal in what must have been an attempt to make him sound "current."

And the lyrics... they all seemed to be about either overcoming great past struggles and being happy now, or about how great things were in the past, but... there was no specificity there. It was all "I tried so hard, and nothing was right/But now I'm back, with you as my wife" and "It was a new wine, a new time, a new day/But now that sunshine's in old times of yesterday." As a writer I had to wince at the mixed metaphors, the clichés, and the utter lack of telling details. As a music listener I was wincing more at the blandness of the music.

I knew one thing. This wasn't the work of a musical genius. This wasn't the work of the man who'd made *Goodbye Dragon*, and it wasn't even the work of the man who'd written "She's My Lady" or "Misty Lady." If it had ever been released, those Cillas fans who thought that Robert was the musical messiah would probably have had the greatest mantitlement strop in history, as they tried to reconcile the evidence of their ears with the unfortunate reality.

There was nothing incriminating about the album's contents, though. No matter how much I listened, I wasn't able to find anything that anyone might have wanted to cover up, or anything that might have led to a murder. No coded confessions of adultery, no between-songs chatter with Robert saying "I have secretly been blackmailing my old friend Mr. Bob Murderer," no evidence whatsoever that the album was anything other than what it sounded like – a generic piece of woeful old-person music, made by some embarrassingly bad songwriters who'd spent a lot of money on having their dull songs played by very expensive dull musicians.

And that meant that I now had a very good idea of who had committed at least one of the murders. What I couldn't figure out is why he'd killed the other two. But I was going to find out.

# You Could Have Told Me

I'd been thinking a lot about the change in musical style between the band's earlier recordings and *Goodbye Dragon*, and about the way Pete had apparently idolised Robert early on and now despised him; about the way that Pete had suddenly quit the band on the day of the album's release and had to sign an NDA, and about the way that Robert had not made a single note of music since Pete quit the band. And about how Pete had been working with Robert in the studio on *Goodbye Dragon*, when all the rest of the band members weren't about.

I'd come to some conclusions and I didn't like them. I decided I needed to speak with Pete, alone and soon. Because if my suspicions were correct, I had a very good idea who had killed Robert, and why.

I called Pete up and asked him to come and meet me. We arranged to meet in a Caffe Nero in the city centre – I wanted somewhere public, because if things turned violent I wanted witnesses around. I didn't think violence was likely, but I've learned not to take risks.

I'd been sat there for about ten minutes, sipping on my soy latte and wondering why the soy milk in chain coffee shops always has that appley aftertaste that it doesn't have when you make the same drinks at home, when Pete finally came in. He ordered his coffee and a muffin, and sat down across the table from me.

"Hey – so, you wanted to meet up? Something on your mind?"

"You could say that. I've been wanting to ask you something – this may sound out of left field, but do you write songs yourself at all?"

He looked puzzled. "I did at one point, but I've not written much recently. Why do you ask?"

"Oh, just something you said during the recording sessions – you talked about wanting the band members to be able to bring in their own songs."

"Did I?" He thought. "Maybe I did. Yeah, it would be nice to have had some creative input into the album. Though then again, right now it'd just be nice to have the album coming out at all, whoever did anything on it. I could really do with the money."

He looked depressed and took a sip of his coffee.

"I don't suppose you have any demos of your stuff?"

He brightened up. "I do actually! I've actually got some of them on my phone!"

He pulled it out and started pulling up apps and scrolling. "I'm sorry, I'm not very good at working these things. Here you go," he passed me his earbuds. "Don't worry, I haven't got any ear infections or anything!"

I laughed. "I wasn't worried until now!"

I put the earbuds in, and listened. It was good. Really, really, good. It was imaginative, complex, a beautiful cascade of counterpoint, but without ever descending into wankery. It was so good, in fact, that it confirmed my worst suspicions. I took the earbuds out.

"That's very interesting," I said to him. "You see, you're talking now about wanting creative input, but of course your only creative input on the Cillas' records was the drum parts. Robert and Ray wrote the songs. So why would you see writing new songs as being a necessary part of having creative input now?"

He looked flustered. "I don't... I'm not... what..."

"Robert and Ray did write the songs, didn't they? And of course, Robert wrote all the songs on *Goodbye Dragon* alone, didn't he? After his songwriting partner Ray had died."

Pete started to pale.

"His songwriting partner Ray, who was in love with him, and who Robert used to treat like shit. His songwriting partner Ray who did all the work and let Robert take equal shares of the credit in order to make Robert like him more."

Pete had actually started to cry.

"So when Robert lost his meal ticket he was desperate, wasn't he? And then he got lucky. He discovered that his drummer – his young, hero-worshipping, drummer – was somehow an even better songwriter than his last 'partner.' And you cared so much about Ray – about all the band members – that you wrote those gorgeous songs about losing him. But Robert got greedy, didn't he? Took all the credit for your collaborations, not just half the credit like he had with Ray. Is that why you quit the band?"

He nodded.

"He threatened you with a lawsuit if you ever told anyone about it, didn't he? Probably also paid you off, a small amount, but in return for you signing an agreement."

"Yeah, I can tell you now, since he's died. I double-checked the terms today, and the agreement only lasted until his death. You're right, he basically didn't write a note of it."

"Not anything?"

"Well, I can't *swear* to you that there's not a single idea he contributed. We'd be in the studio together, and I'd lay down all these tracks – guitar, piano, drums, cello, whatever – I learned half of the instruments while we were recording, just well enough to get the ideas down, you know? If there's a cello in the studio you have a crack at it. Well, he'd be there, and he might say 'go du du du du du instead of takatakataka' or something, so there might be some of his ideas in there. But really, he was just watching me do all the work."

"How about the collaborations with Ray? Do you think Robert actually contributed to them?"

"Well, none of us can know for sure, but my guess knowing them both is that Ray wrote everything. I mean, it makes sense, right? Ray loved him so much, and would do anything for him. And also... I mean, you don't know what Robert was like, but he had this sort of overbearing personality, and he could make everything seem like his idea even when it wasn't."

I nodded slowly, imagining this.

"I can easily believe that him and Ray would go into a room together, Ray would pick up the guitar and write the song, and Robert would make just enough suggestions that he could convince Ray – and maybe even himself – that he was an equal partner in the writing."

I took another sip of my latte, just to break eye contact for a while. All of this was sounding so intense.

"And by the time they brought the songs to the rest of us, they were presented as stuff that Robert had come up with, with maybe a little help from Ray. It was a subtle thing, but I'm absolutely convinced the man has never written a song in his life." Pete sighed. "And the thing is, the others actually never realised this. I mean, as soon as I got annoyed with him, that was it, I was sacked from the band by lawyers' letter the next day."

"I thought you quit."

"That was part of the deal in the NDA. I was sacked, for wanting my share of the credit."

"I... I don't believe all this. That doesn't make any sense. Surely you told the other band members you wrote the songs?"

"No. That's the thing I still don't completely understand about my own behaviour. But Robert referred to them as 'our songs' when he was telling the band about them, and even when we were talking together in the studio. And I suppose I still believed in the myth that had got me into the band in the first place, that he was this big genius. So they were 'our songs', not 'my songs that Robert added fuck all to.' And I didn't see that he'd left me off the credits until the day the album itself came out. I blew up at him, and got a letter from his lawyers by special delivery the next morning.

"I'm sure he told the others the opposite of the truth – that *he'd* been the one who was being polite to *me* and saying the songs were ours when really they were just his. He'll probably have said that he was going to cut me in on the royalties at first, for all my 'help' in the studio, but that I'd been an arse to him and he'd decided against it. I know him well enough to know that's exactly the kind of line he'd spin.

"It's not the money I really care about, or even the credit as such – those songs were important to me, they were about my dead mate."

I nodded. "And presumably that's why *Rising Up* was never finished, and why Robert never wrote any more songs after that – those were all your songs as well?"

"I'd guess so. I mean, I don't know – I literally never spoke to him from the day I was fired until he turned up again after Graham's death – but those were my songs, yeah, and I don't think any of the others in the band wrote. So yeah, that's the secret of the Great Lost Album," he pronounced the capitals, "it woz the drummer wot dun it."

(I wondered briefly if the drummer had done anything else, but put my suspicions out of my head for the moment. I was there to collect information, not to shout "j'accuse!")

"So why didn't you ever make any more music yourself?"

He took a sip of his coffee and smiled grimly. "The legal agreement forbade me from making any more music for at least five years. I guess he didn't want anyone hearing what I'd done and making the connection." He sighed. "But also... it's not like the record labels were clamouring to give contracts to a young kid who'd been the replacement drummer in a mid-tier glam band. The executives were doing a lot of coke in those days, but not enough to see that as a major commercial proposition."

He took another sip of coffee, and then shook his head. "But no, the truth is, I was just fucking sick of it. I'd only been in the music business a couple of years, and I'd had me songs stolen off me by my biggest idol, who'd sacked me. My other idol, who'd been a mate as well as someone I admired, had died."

He took a deep breath, slowly.

I wondered if he was done talking but before I could think of anything to say, he went on. "And the industry was full of fucking monsters. I mean, you know about Glitter and Savile and that fucker who managed the Rollers... and our manager was just as bad. I'm not a religious man, but I sometimes hope there's a hell, just so Clive Salisbury gets what he deserves.

"No, the question isn't why I quit the music industry," he swigged the rest of his coffee down in one gulp, "it's why I ever thought it was a good idea to come back." He put his coffee cup on the table. "See ya."

He went out the door, leaving his untouched muffin behind.

# Make Me Smile (Come Up and See Me)

I went back home from Birmingham that evening, and spent the next couple of days thinking. I'd formed a pretty good idea of who I thought was committing these murders, and I was fairly confident I had some ideas about why.

What I wasn't entirely sure of was whether or not the band members were actually telling the truth. Not only was there the possibility that one of them might be the murderer, but it also might be the case that decades of talking about the same events over and over might have eroded their memories – as a reporter, I'm very aware that after a while people remember the story they're used to telling much better than they remember the actual events they created the story about, often without knowing that's what they're doing.

People like Beth and Claire would probably know more of the truth than the band members, at this point, but there was one person I could be sure would be able to give me the facts I needed to ensure that there wasn't a vital hole in my timeline – Chuck.

Beth and Claire were fans of the story of the band at least as much as they were fans of the band that really existed, and that kind of creative fandom culture, while wonderful, is much more aligned with the "best story" version of events. Chuck, on the other hand, was the kind of fact-obsessed creeper who would have a complete list of every band member's middle name, email password, National Insurance number and blood type somewhere, so it was him I needed to turn to.

Luckily Chuck was pretty much always available to talk to. He seemed to have no life at all outside of the band – I wasn't sure where he got his money from, or what kind of lifestyle he had, because he never, ever talked about anything other than the band and his religion, but I got the impression that his life didn't involve much human contact. I didn't even know where he lived, but he said he was hanging around in London for the moment, to attend the funeral and "comfort the other people in the organisation." I had a sneaking suspicion that this would mean trying to steal bits of the body and then livestreaming the funeral on Twitter, but I didn't say anything.

As I had to travel to London as well, to sort out business stuff with the band's management – I was clearly not going to get paid the full amount for a tour that had never really got started, but nor was Jane, and we needed to negotiate getting as much as possible of that money if we were going to last until we could pick up new jobs – I arranged to meet up with him in a greasy spoon cafe near where he was staying in Hackney. Of course, when I got there there was no vegan food on the menu – I suspected even the toast would probably be smeared with lard – so I sipped on a horrible instant coffee while he wolfed down black pudding.

"So how did you actually become a fan of the Cillas? I mean, you weren't even born when they were having their success."

"I read an article in *Mojo* about Robert. And... something about him touched me. His life paralleled mine in so many ways. He was the person I saw myself as becoming, really. He was the person I wanted to make myself into. And the music, when I heard *Goodbye Dragon* especially... that was even better than the music I'd imagined when I'd read about him. It was obvious that he was writing the soundtrack for my life. I don't want to make it sound like I think that was deliberate – it's just that there are parallels, you know? Did you ever find anything like that, where the life of a writer or a musician infused their work?"

I nodded. I'd felt that kind of thing a lot over the years.

"So it wasn't the other Cillas you were particularly bothered by? Just Robert?"

"Well, they're the same thing really, aren't they? Robert never made any records without the Cillas, and he wrote all their songs. He was the only one who was even on all the records."

"Other than Graham of course."

He waved a hand dismissively. "Oh yeah, well, Graham. He was a perfectly decent singer, and I don't like to speak ill of him after he's passed on, but he was never really someone who *understood* the Cillas. He didn't get what it was that made them special, you know?"

"You mean he thought it was him that made the Cillas special?"

He laughed. "That was part of it, no doubt. But it was more than that. Have you heard any of his solo stuff? None of it has the same feel as the Cillas' records. You could imagine Rod Stewart or Elton John or any of a dozen other people singing those songs."

"And you don't think that's the case with the Cillas' stuff?"

He looked shocked. "Gosh no! Have you not listened to it? It's a totally different experience to anything any of those guys could do. I mean, when did any of them ever write a song like 'Kiss Me, Galileo'?"

"But the song's not everything, is it? A record is different from just the sheet music to the song."

He thought for a second. "I know what you mean, but it's still fundamentally about the song for me. You could have a totally different band from the Cillas playing those songs and they'd still be great, but if you get the Cillas covering someone else's song... well, I'd listen to it, because I'd want to see what they did with the arrangement and stuff, but it wouldn't be as good as them doing their own work."

"You say 'their own,' but of course you mean Robert's songs."

He paused. "Well... yes. That's what I mean I suppose."

"So if they do anything together now that Robert's dead, you won't listen to it?"

"I didn't say that. They're talented people. They might surprise us, you never know. But it's the classic music I'm most interested in. And really only *Goodbye Dragon*. The rest of it's fun enough, but *that's* the music I care about. I'd definitely listen if there was a good chance of them coming up with something that sounded like that."

"And you think there is a chance, even though Robert's dead?"

He looked flustered. "I didn't say that, either. I'm just interested in what they do. Obviously since Robert was the credited songwriter on everything on *Goodbye Dragon*, there's not going to be anything that sounds like that, unless one of them has learned how to imitate him really well by playing his music."

"How about the new album they were working on? Do you want them to finish that?"

He waved his hand, "Nah, it's pretty much finished already. I've got what they'd already done, and it's not up to Robert's usual standard. It doesn't deserve releasing. It'd only harm the legacy. Best to let the band be remembered for their great work in the 70s."

And now I knew for sure exactly who had committed the murders.

# Pride Comes Before a Fall

Chuck was talking about the album as if he knew it very well. Yet he'd never been in any of the sessions. The album had never come out. How could he have heard the album at all, let alone have such casual knowledge of it? As far as I was aware, I was the only person other than the band and Jeffrey who'd heard it. So how could he have possibly formed any opinion of it at all?

Except that the copy that had been earmarked for Jeffrey had disappeared, and I'd guessed that maybe the murderer had taken it. Things were starting to come together in my head. I was forming suspicions I didn't want to voice. At least not yet. But I had to ask him some more questions, before I could confirm them.

"So you've heard the new album?"

He looked flustered for a brief second, as if he wasn't expecting the question at all. He recovered quickly, though, and answered as if he hadn't been thrown at all.

"Oh yeah. I mean, it was largely done even before Jeffrey died. I got Robert to dump the rough mixes to CD for me, so I could have a copy for my archives of the work-in-progress. Which, I guess, was a good idea given what happened to him later."

That almost sounded plausible. Almost. But then I thought... he asked Robert to dump the rough mixes to CD? Robert who didn't have the first clue about any recording technology since the days of mono? This wasn't adding up at all... or rather, it was adding up to something very unpleasant indeed. Something I was going to have to tread carefully around.

"So what did you think of it?"

"Well, I'm not ever going to say anything against Robert's genius, you understand, but... it wasn't worthy of him, and certainly not worthy of being the Cillas' reunion album. It would have spoiled the legacy if it had come out."

That was pretty much exactly what I'd guessed. This talk of archives and legacies was making everything very clear to me.

"What do you mean, if it had come out? Surely they can still release it?"

"The multitracks were wiped. Robert was working on them when he was killed, and they were deleted."

This was the first I'd heard of this, and I wondered who could have wiped them, what possible motive they could have had, and most of all how Chuck would know about that. Unless it had been him who'd wiped them.

"But you've got that rough mix CD. They could use that, couldn't they?"

"You can't just release rough mixes! You surely can't mean that?"

I didn't know what I meant, but his defensiveness about releasing the recording was ringing alarm bells.

"Why not? If it's good enough for you to listen to, surely it's good enough for other people?"

"But... but... but they're..."

"Yours?"

"No! No, I don't mean that! I just mean that there are things that are okay for the fans and things that are okay for the public, and those are two different things. It's just the way things are. Fans understand the band in a way that the general public don't. You have to have something clean and polished, or the band will get embarrassed by it!"

"But Robert can't get embarrassed any more, can he? He's dead, remember?"

"But there's his reputation to uphold!"

"His reputation as someone who hasn't released an album in forty-odd years?"

"No! His reputation as a musical genius! He deserves only his best work to go out there! Anything else just wouldn't be respectful!"

Something was clearly panicking Chuck, and I wanted to figure out what it is.

"So you're not going to play any of the tracks on your podcast then?"

"I would never... never... not this."

"You're sure of that?"

"Of course! I'm not going to spread the rough mixes of an unreleased album on my podcast! That would be... it would be desecration of the band's legacy!"

"But you've shared plenty of rough mixes of stuff from the *Rising Up* sessions on your podcast. That was far more unfinished than this new album was."

"That's different, though. Those mixes are already out there – people have been trading the tapes since the eighties, and half of all the Cillanites out there have put out their own fan edits trying to complete it. That material's already in the public domain."

My inner intellectual-property law pedant winced at the misuse of "public domain" for material that was very definitely in copyright, but there was no point getting into that. "But don't you think you perhaps owe it to the fandom, the people who shared those other bootlegs with you, to share this with them? I'm not saying you should, just trying to understand the thought process."

He started to redden. "No. No I don't owe them anything. I have my sources for that music, and those sources chose to share it with me. I was never under any obligation to share anything back – and by doing so I would lessen the music's value. What if someone wanted to share an unheard song from the *Goodbye Dragon* sessions with me? They wouldn't do it if they knew I was the kind of person who'd make everything he had public. And what if they would only share it if I gave them something they didn't already have? If I didn't have these recordings, I wouldn't be able to bargain with them. But more importantly, there's the band's legacy to consider."

"You keep talking about the legacy, what do you mean?"

"I mean what I say you stupid bitch. The body of work is too important to have it desecrated by this. They should go down in history as a band that made three perfect albums and one unfinished masterpiece, not three perfect albums, an unfinished masterpiece, and a half-arsed piece of shit! I'm protecting them, and you'd better do the same!"

I'd always thought Chuck was a nasty piece of shit, but this was confirming it. Still, I needed to know if he was threatening me or just being a prick.

"What do you mean, I'd better do the same?"

"I know you have a copy. Scott at the studio told me you'd taken one." He smiled smugly. "You thought no-one had noticed, did you? People pay more attention to you than you think. I told him to call the police on you, but he refused to take my advice. Said it wouldn't hurt anything. But since the recordings have been wiped, I know that you have the only copy other than mine anywhere. You won't be able to resist the temptation to make yourself big in fan circles – you want to get that rep that people like me have taken years to build up. You'll be sticking the files up on a private server somewhere, and sharing the passwords with the highest bidder."

I boggled at the idea that I could actually care about my reputation in Cillas fandom. But then, if you're a big fish in the tiniest possible pond, the idea that other people could be thinking in terms of the ocean is probably an unusual one.

He seemed to realise himself that he was going slightly over the top, and calmed down a little. "Look, all I'm asking is that you think about the band's reputation among future generations. You know them, you like them. Do you really want them to be viewed as a bunch of lazy has-been hacks when they could be remembered as the great artists they were?"

Again, I thought all this talk of posterity and future generations was slightly risible. After all, we were talking about a minor glam rock band here, somewhere below Slade, Wizzard, or T-Rex but above the Glitter Band and the Sweet in the glam rock hierarchy, not the bloody Beatles – although I had to admit that the strength of feeling among the fandom, and the size of the audiences, was much greater than I'd imagined it would be.

I thought about how much I cared about my own fandoms, and about the more toxic men in it.

And I realised that I had to get away from this man, at least for the moment. Talking to him any more in private would do nothing.

"Look, I promise you – I swear on Jane's life – that I will not be sharing those tracks with anyone. You can trust me on this."

I must have looked convincing, because he stared at me for a moment, and then nodded.

"Very well. I trust I shall be seeing you at the funeral tomorrow?"

I told him he would. I had plans.

# Roll Away the Stone

I've never been much of one for funerals at the best of times. Even when it's someone who died in their bed aged ninety-five, you don't want to go to see them be set on fire or dumped in the ground, while lots of people stand around and cry.

But Jane felt like we had to show our faces at Robert's funeral, so off we went, in black dresses and sombre faces, to say goodbye to someone neither of us particularly liked or knew all that well. But at least we weren't alone in that. Of all the people there, maybe ten wanted to deal with their grief over Robert's death. The rest were mostly seeing it as some kind of networking opportunity.

It was disgusting, but then that's the kind of thing I'd come to expect from the music business.

What was surprising was how many faces I recognised. Along with the band, and people in their circle like Green, there seemed to be quite a few familiar faces I knew from TV and the news. A few old 70s pop stars, a couple of music business people and DJs... more disgraced former stars than I'd have thought, too. I'd have thought that more of the Yewtree lot would have had a sense of shame and not shown themselves in public, but apparently they all wanted to schmooze with their showbiz pals like it was still 1974. I was half surprised that Gary Glitter wasn't there – he'd have fit right in with this lot.

But I got over my sense of visceral disgust at being in a gang of 1970s showbiz people, and started to mingle as we waited outside for the church doors to open. I wasn't going to talk with the dirty old men, obviously, but I thought I'd at least have a chat with the band.

None of them seemed devastated with loss, understandably enough, and they were talking business, but at least they weren't ostentatiously glad-handing record company executives, just having the same kind of discussions among themselves about what they could do next that Jane and I had been having. I couldn't blame them for that – they needed to eat, and their pension plan had just been comprehensively fucked over.

"So can the tour even possibly continue at this point?" Pete was asking.

"No. There's just no way," replied Terry. "I mean, think about it. We never even played together before this year. Robert and Graham were the glue holding the band together, and they're both gone now. It's like this band is fucking jinxed."

"I'm not sure," said Sid. "I mean, yes, we have to cancel *this* tour – we can't go out there and play the fucking Hammersmith Apollo when we haven't got a lead singer. But we can do something together, I'm sure. I mean, the three of us have been getting on pretty well, I think, and it wasn't like Robert or Graham were ever really one of the gang, was it? I know they were the pretty boys, but that was forty years ago. No-one's going to be coming to see us to lust over us, are they?"

"You've got a point, I suppose," said Terry. "Look, I'll think about it, but I can't say more than that. I really don't know what's been happening here, and it's like we're in bloody Spinal Tap, except it's lead singers keep popping off instead of drummers."

At this point, at some signal I didn't see but which everyone seemed to agree on, we all started walking inside.

It was a strange old church – the building itself seemed to be bent, with the back half not quite at the same angle as the front. I later found out that there was an old legend that the Devil had come to town and lifted up the church by its back, but that the vicar had come out and forced the Devil to drop it by sheer force of holiness. The Devil had dropped it, but it had been left at an angle.

Personally, I thought it was more likely that the people who'd built it had all been pissed out of their heads, but that's just me.

I had to admit, though, that the inside of the church was quite beautiful. There was no artificial illumination at all – all the light came through the stained glass windows, so the room was dappled with different colours. And there was a wonderful acoustic resonance to the space – I could see Jane was itching to have a go on the church organ, which was being played rather badly, and to put it through its paces.

Instead of taking over the organ, though, she sat on a bench at the back and I joined her. I tried to figure out what the music was that the organist was playing – it wasn't any of the normal hymns or funeral marches you'd expect, and it took a while before I twigged.

"That's 'Misty Lady'! I whispered to Jane. "They're playing a song about having sex with an old woman, at his funeral!"

She nodded. "His wife chose it, apparently. She said it was his favourite of the songs he'd written, and it would be an appropriate way to honour him."

I didn't correct her on who had written the song, of course. Not the time or place for that conversation.

"But... it's about being a gerontophile! Could you get more inappropriate?"

"You're right. But then, Robert was hardly the most appropriate of people, was he?"

I had to admit that that was true. I was going to get into more discussion of funeral music, but then I noticed the murmur of the crowd hushed and the coffin was carried in. The three surviving band members were pallbearers, pushing the coffin in on a trolley, along with Andy, Chuck, and Scott the engineer. How sad, I thought, that none of his friends or family were there for this, just work colleagues who didn't like him very much.

And then I had to stifle a laugh, thinking that they'd carried him all through his life, and now they were carrying him in death.

But Chuck was there. Chuck. A pallbearer. And I just broke.

I'd been planning on confronting him afterwards, at the wake – somewhere public, yes, but not in the actual funeral. But I couldn't stand the sight of that man carrying his victim, so I just stood up and screamed.

"How dare you? How dare you pretend to mourn him? Murderer!"

# Own Up, Take a Look at Yourself

"What?"

"You heard. You murdered Robert. Murderer!"

The congregation were deathly quiet at this point. You could have heard a pin drop. Everyone had turned to look at Chuck, who was turning red with fury.

What could I do? I had no proof. I knew what had happened, but there was no physical evidence at all. It was just the only thing that made sense of everything I knew.

But I knew what I had to do. His attitude to religion had given me the clue. While he was standing there, red-faced, surrounded on all sides by shouting mourners, I managed to push out of the crowd and ran down the aisle of the church toward the pulpit. I grabbed the Bible from the lectern, and brought it back towards Chuck. I'm pretty sure he figured out then what I was planning, and his face paled. But he still continued with his bluster.

"What the he— what do you think you're doing? This is a church, a house of God, and...what are you doing? This is a funeral!"

"I know it is, and I'm bringing you to justice, in the sight of the people who loved the man you killed." That was probably an exaggeration – with the exception of Kate, I don't know if anyone there loved him. Well, except Chuck himself, of course. "Swear on the Bible that you didn't do it, if you didn't."

"What? That's absurd!"

"Go on. Take that Bible in your hands and swear on it. Just do it. It's that simple."

He continued looking at the Bible, and I could see a few beads of sweat forming on his forehead.

"That's all you have to do. Just take the Bible, swear on it that you didn't murder Robert Michaels. In fact, tell you what, just swear on it that you didn't murder Graham or Jeffrey if you'd prefer. Can you honestly swear, on your immortal soul, that you killed none of them?"

"This is absurd, and I won't stand for any of this nonsense! This is just abuse, and I won't dignify your... your blasphemy!"

"So swearing on the Bible is blasphemy now?"

"You're standing in a holy place, Sarah. You're making false accusations against me. Thou shalt not bear false witness – but that's exactly what you're doing. You're evil."

"If I'm bearing false witness, there's an easy way to prove it. All you have to do is swear, on your Bible, by your God, that you didn't kill anyone. If you're so keen on your commandments, you should remember that one. Thou shalt not kill. Or doesn't that one count for you?"

At this point the vicar had come over – she was looking furious at the commotion.

"What on Earth is all this? This is a funeral, show some respect!"

I turned to her. "Look, I'm truly, truly sorry about this. I would never normally disrespect a holy place or a dead person. But I am convinced – utterly, totally convinced – that this man here murdered Robert Michaels. If I'm right, it would be a far greater disrespect to his memory to let this man sit here and pretend to mourn him."

She turned to look at Chuck. "Is this true?"

"Of course it's not true. She's a fucking psycho bitch!"

At this point, the vicar actually lunged at Chuck, but Jane put her arm out, and pulled the vicar to one side, while Chuck continued. Meanwhile, several of the congregation, seeing him blustering, had moved to block his exit. And most of the rest were taking video with their phones. This was far more entertainment than they'd expected.

"I have never killed anyone. I'd never even hurt anyone! All I want to do is sit at home and listen to my Cillas records. I am literally the most harmless person you will ever meet."

"Tell that to Beth and Claire."

He boggled. "What?"

"Beth and Claire. You ripped off their websites for your own. You spread false rumours about them. You took over their fandom from them."

"Their fandom?"

"Yes, theirs." It felt like such a surreal argument to be getting in, in a lovely old church where I'd just interrupted a funeral. But right now, nothing could stop me. "They'd built this little space for themselves on the Internet, to talk to their friends about an old band they loved, and you came along with your need for everything to be serious and important and... *man.* You made the fandom a safe space for boring straight boring white men and their boring beards, at the expense of everyone else. You forced them out of their hobby and you didn't even notice you'd done it. You're fucking *toxic.*"

"I never wanted to force anyone out. And I'm not going to apologise for getting the Cillas' music some respect at last. It's too important to be treated like trash. And none of that makes me a murderer."

"You've still not sworn on the Bible that you're not."

"This is fucking ridiculous." He turned to the people blocking his way. "Let me out. I'm not sticking around here to be accused of these monstrous crimes." He turned back to me. "I'll be suing you for slander. You'll be hearing from my lawyers – and I have very good ones."

"I'm sure you do. You'll have to swear on a Bible if you take me to court, you know."

Jane was pulling on my sleeve, trying to pull me away, but I shook her off. The funeral had already been completely disrupted. I continued talking, getting louder and louder over the commotion of the crowd.

"You killed them all. You killed Graham because you knew he and Robert wouldn't ever be on stage together, and it was the only way to get Robert back in the band."

"This is –"

"Then you killed Jeffrey because you thought he was ruining Robert's music, making it into bland pap. You thought that with him gone, you'd finally get another album of genius. But then you heard Pete and Robert talking, and you realised that Pete had written all Robert's songs. And so you killed Robert out of revenge for him having lied all those years."

Chuck turned red and screamed "No, you *fucking bitch!* I killed him to protect his reputation!"

The crowd went very quiet.

"How do you think he would have felt, knowing that everyone knew he'd faked everything? I wasn't a fan of the *music*, I was a fan of *him!* It was his *life* that had spoken to me! His struggle! And if it had ever come out that he'd not made the music, then he... everyone would just have dismissed him! I did it for him!"

He turned away from me and toward the other mourners. "I'm the only one of you who actually cared about the man, not just some shitting songs! You should be thanking me for trying to protect him! Fucking ingrates!"

He dropped to his knees, by the coffin, which was still resting on the trolley which the pallbearers had been pushing, and started to cry. "Why couldn't you have just stayed retired?" He kept asking, over and over, until the police finally arrived.

# Rock and Roll (Part 2)

At least the trial came quickly. The murders had taken place in late October, and by mid February I was testifying. I suppose when the murderer confesses in front of a couple of hundred people, the wheels of justice don't have to grind all that slowly.

And so I found myself at the Old Bailey (which it turns out is an actual real place and not just something you get in old TV shows) being a witness.

The trial... well, here I was for the second time in a year, testifying about a murder case. It's not a position I'm at all comfortable in – my job as a reporter is to tell people what's going on, and being a witness in a criminal case is sort of similar to that, but the difference there is that the focus is on you, not on the story.

And in other ways, it's more like being an interview subject, but not a friendly interview. You get the same kind of probing questions and attempts to find holes in your story that... well, that I'd used on Chuck and the band members to try and find out who the killer was. It made me wonder about the ethics of my own work, in a way that I never had before.

But then, on the other hand, it was all about bringing a murderer to justice – a murderer I'd caught – so was that ethical justification for my own work? I wasn't sure, especially since my feelings about the justice system are mixed at best. But I did know that having been responsible for him being caught, I also had a responsibility, both to society and the truth, to stand up there in front of everyone and tell the truth as best I could. That's also why I write these books, even though I'd rather be writing reviews of the latest piece of Apple kit or something.

I was worried that I was being forced into crime journalism. But still, if I'd failed at the showbiz and tech fields, at least crime offered definite possibilities. You don't have to explain much jargon to people when you just say "Mr. X smashed Mr. Y over the head with a hammer."

But the whole thing was mystifying to me. Why had I been involved in two separate cases of multiple murders in a year? What had I done to deserve that? No, don't answer that, it's not the kind of question you want an answer for.

The people I felt sorriest for in all this were the band members. Twice now their careers had been fucked over by other people's egos. They'd done nothing to deserve any of it. I hoped that Terry, Sid, and Pete were okay. I mean, I know they weren't exactly devastated over Robert on a personal level, but seeing people you work with being murdered is going to rattle you no matter how you feel about them. I knew that well enough by now, certainly.

And Pete was a genuinely great songwriter who'd had his greatest work stolen from him, and all of them had been conned out of royalties they'd deserved far more than the stupid waster who'd kept the money for himself.

And poor Ray. Obviously I'd never met him, but I couldn't help feeling for him most of all. He'd so obviously loved Robert, and I don't know if Robert had ever even realised. I don't know what would be worse – to have known Ray loved him and deliberately used him because of that, or to have been so self-absorbed that you could sit there while someone poured out song after song about his love for you, blatant stuff like "If only you could see me" and "Though I'll never tell you, you're the one," and not even realise that was what he was doing.

It would be nice to believe in some sort of natural justice, but nobody had come out of this with what they deserved. Robert had destroyed people's lives, but he hadn't deserved to die. And Graham and Jeffrey had been completely innocent bystanders, just trying to make a living. Chuck thought they were obstacles in the same way he thought I wanted to get big in Cillas fandom: these things only ever made sense inside his head, and Graham and Jeffrey could never have known the parts they played in his weird calculations.

So the only thing I could do was to support some *un*natural justice, some human justice, even if I don't support the carceral system and even if reliving some pretty fucking traumatic events was not very far from giving me PTSD.

At least I didn't have to testify on a Bible. As an atheist, I affirmed and attested, internally relieved that I didn't have to relive that bit quite so viscerally.

Chuck, who represented himself of course, his boasts about expensive lawyers having been just part of his bluster, refused to testify at all. In fact, he stated he was going to "take the fifth", which suggests that he really didn't truly understand that he was in the UK and not the USA at all.

Just another example of his weird privileged attitude that placed the things he was interested in at the centre of the world, and anything he wasn't interested in as an utter irrelevance to which he needed to pay no attention at all. It didn't matter to him that the UK has a different legal system than what he'd read or heard about from American TV shows or much of the internet. Over here, unlike there, staying silent can be used as evidence of guilt.

But yeah, privilege came up against public law and, for once, public law won. Chuck actually got sent to a secure mental hospital to serve out his sentence. There was a discussion in the trial between experts for the defence and the prosecution as to what his actual mental condition was, but everyone agreed he had something. That made me feel really sorry for him, surprisingly enough. I once knew someone who worked in one of those places as a nurse, and from what he said the conditions there are much, much worse than they are in a prison.

Beth and Claire actually came to the trial and watched most of it from the public galleries. I was surprised, really – they hadn't liked Robert that much, and they certainly didn't like Chuck, and they had (quite rightly) regarded the murders as something horrific they'd like to put out of their minds, rather than as an exciting adventure to relive.

I chatted to them after I testified, though, and they told me that they felt it was the only decent thing to do, to honour the three men who had been killed by another member of their fandom. They felt a responsibility to at least find out the facts as they stood in the trial, and to remember, and to let other people know in the fandom context, rather than having their friends just find out from the news reports. They're actually far more serious minded than I'd given them credit for – it turned out that even as I'd been admiring them I'd also been patronising them a little. It's a hard thing, to get rid of that little internal voice that tells you young women have nothing to offer, even if you're a young woman yourself.

And after the trial, I could go home, and finally try to put all of this behind us.

We've never been big ones for celebrating Valentine's Day normally, but this year felt like a bit of a special one, so we'd decided to at least have a nice dinner at home. We dressed up, lit a few candles, placed strategically not so much for the brightness as to be out of easy reach of the cat, and tried to have a proper romantic time together for the first time in months.

Over dinner, Jane told me what she'd learned from the Cillas' management.

"So the Cillas are going to continue touring – just Pete, Sid, and Terry. They're going to go out on an I Love The 70s package tour next winter with Suzi Quattro, the Bay City Rollers, Tenpole Tudor and the bass player from the Jam. They can't afford me and Simon, but I'm glad they're doing something at least."

I thought about what that would involve.

"But that's shit! You can't tell me that those three expect to actually play their own instruments, without anyone to cover for them?"

"Oh no. On those package tours you have one band that backs all the solo singers and vocal groups. They'll just come out and stand in front of the backing band and do their vocals in matching suits."

"That's a real comedown from playing full shows by themselves for their own screaming fans, isn't it?"

"That's the way these things work. I've done those jobs myself, so I know how it goes. It's shit, but at least they'll keep on getting paid for making music, and really they'll get a reasonable whack for fifteen minutes or half an hour's work a night."

I thought about Terry, Pete and Sid, going out every night and singing their hits with a cheesy backing band, and maybe with Andy along to impersonate Graham or Robert. Odd as it seemed, I thought they'd probably like that. They were working men, and they'd be earning a living, supporting their families, all that stuff that's so important to men of that generation.

"They'd still have to do the bloody Christmas song, though, wouldn't they?"

"I'm afraid they would."

"What about the name, though? Don't Robert and Graham's wives own that?"

"I expect they'll figure out that getting some money from licensing the name is better than getting no money from it. Especially Kate, if Pete points out to her that he could sue for songwriting royalties for *Goodbye Dragon*."

So it wasn't a perfect happy ending for them, but at least they'd get something.

And I'd got something as well. I'd got my name on the front pages of all the newspapers, and they were talking about me as some kind of super-sleuth. It felt weird, but almost good. I mean, there was the obvious disadvantage that in order to get this reputation as a fantastic supergenius I'd had to be around a lot of really grim stuff that I'd never be able to get out of my dreams, but the truth was I had been able to help find and stop murderers, and it's really nice to be recognised as actually good at something that helps people.

This had been a hard winter, after a hard summer before that, but Jane and I had got through it together, and things were only going to get better over the next year. I promised myself that much. We were going to have the best 2019 ever.

(I may have been a little drunk, or I wouldn't have put it that way, even in my head.)

What I needed more than anything was for the rest of the year to be different. "I'm thinking of trying my hand at something else," I said. "Working as a PR flak is clearly not the right job for me. The last thing I need is to be writing happy, jolly, material about bosses. I'm thinking of getting into writing opinion stuff."

"I can see that," Jane said. "Only thing is, how will you possibly develop any opinions, what with you being so demure and all?"

I threw a bread roll at her, and she laughed.

"I know. It seems like the obvious role for me. Start writing political opinions, maybe do a little investigative journalism? I should try to get a press pass for the political conferences."

She raised an eyebrow. "Really? Political conferences? Have you been to any of them?"

"I know... I know you used to be in the Greens, and keep telling me how incredibly boring it was. But I honestly think it could be fun. All that drinking and debauchery and scandal..."

"You have no idea what actually happens at a political conference do you?"

"I do so! I've watched every episode of *The Thick of It!*"

"Only because you fancy Rebecca Front."

"That's hardly my point."

We giggled together like schoolchildren. These were always the best times we had, making plans for the future. At times like this, anything seemed possible.

"But we still have to find you another steady gig," I pointed out. "After all, the tour's been cancelled, and you need to be doing something."

"I'll find something soon enough," she said. "I'm good enough at this now that there's always work available."

"Anyway, fancy a quick Valentine's Day snog?"

I'll leave it there, I think. What happened next is our business. But even without her stage costume, Jane's never looked more glamorous than she did that Valentine's Day.

Printed in Great Britain
by Amazon

30870797R00112